AF272576

Dan's adventure in Africa

Arrival at the fort

Shadows flew through the evening light, bizarre, devoured, threateningly deep, over the dry, glowing prairie. Bats. The steppe begins the second life. A hyena, with her gruesome laughing concert and a vulture fought in the distance for her dead prey. Drums shake the whole Ground, so that even a pack of lions force themselves to leave. As unsuspectingly a trek where pushed through the African nightlife. Disempowered by the journey, the whole miserable looking crowd of people is struggling to still reach there goal.

Suddenly the vultures appear in their horizon of vision and even the last ones become restless without seeing it first.

"That's why the drums," said Fernandes called Fed, one of the riders patrol.

"Yes," assessing for a moment, "it's the fort," came it further from the Leader.

"We're too late. If they where more, they might have changed their minds," Fed.

Silently the two blond broad-shouldered rode down the trek to show the people safety again. But the fear was there. They knew it was somewhere on the target. None of them knew exactly what to expect. They wondered if it was in the fort or how the others would welcome them.

They had given up everything and now? Maybe the end of the line? Tom the trekking guide rode, with Fed a little ahead. Actually Fernandes is also one of the trek people, a Spaniard who married an Englishwoman and went with an 8 year old son only to Africa, because of the already 100 years long tensions of the naval forces.

Tom was English who lived in Africa for 20 years and was politically completely uninterested, he just kept scolding the Queen. Because she's not sending troops to protect the settler for political reasons. It wasn't really bearable yet.

"There are actually only two enemies here, great ones you can't learn anything against, death and again death". Tom raised after long silence.

It was now long since they became friends, Fed asked surprised. "How so"?

"There's nothing you can do about the drought and the `black people´." Tom.

- Silence. -

"If the drought hasn't gotten rid of, the 'blacks' will get." Tom.

"Why do the 'blacks' take the dead into there camp?" Fed.

Slightly smiling at his friend's frightenedness Tom responded .

"No don't worry they don't do what its said of them, eating people, but they don't even keep a dog alive. They are afraid that the spirit will enter in any living being influenced by 'whites' and bring in new 'whites'. Because they kept coming back".

They laughed for a moment, then they got serious again.

Since the sun had already set so far, torches were lit.

Dan the son of Fernandes brought them two torches.

Shocked, the father asked, "You're not asleep yet, but now you go - and thank you", and stroked his light-blond hair.

When the boy was gone again, Fed raised again. "And they don't realize that the stream won't stop?"

"Yes - now it's "tradition," we would call it." Tom.

"Awful." Fed.

"This is how every people does it, here it is called barbarism, elsewhere more civilized 'war'". Tom.

"And you?" asked Fed.

"I call it a pointless waste of time, with the side effects, of no overpopulation of the earth," Tom.

"Tom how did you survived 20 years here," Fed.

"In the summer I am on the coast, in winter I sometimes lead people into the country or work as a trader to secure my life. Are you smarter now"? Tom.

He didn't like saying it, like he wasn't comfortable with it.

Then they only talked with individual sentences thrown into the silence. Tom said hard,

"Fernandes you have become my friend with your family. I tell you, your wife knows, it's not staying with the others until it's too late. They themselves have become like beasts on the ship when something happens it becomes dangerous, especially when they start to regret it, - because you led them with me. Believe me."

Meanwhile a few hours had passed and the two riders recognized already the first dead on which the vultures raged, even the hyenas, seemed to have found their victims without fight.

Tom signaled to stop and rode with Fernandes ahead.

After a few shots, the vultures screamed and fled, the hyenas they shot death.

"What now," asks Fed.

In front of them was a fort littered with corpses, none of which could be identified, so they looked.

"Well, what now, we can't go in today," Tom "Let's keep them resting there till tomorrow"? - said Fed questioning.

"Yeah, but someone got to keep a watch here over night"- Tom

"I'll do it you have to get back to the trek," Fed.

"Thanks i´ll be with your family," Tom.

"OK", Fed

"Start a fire, and if you shoot, some one of us will come. Keep the fire up! - Do you still have coffee?" Tom asked, explaining, showing that he didn't really like it.

"Yes, thanks." They hugged each other and Tom rode back.

Back he was already surrounded by everyone, because everyone had heard the shots and asked confusedly what was going on in the fort and where was Fernandes. Tom told everything, had let build a wagon circle and set up guardians.

The night passed without further incidents, accompanied by the drums of the natives.

A horrible sight

The next morning the trek started with the first rays of sunlight. The drumming sounded and there was a stiff silence if it hadn't been disturbed by some returning night hunters.

But after half an hour they stopped and realized that the dead had to be buried first. Since it was felt better for the children, they did not yet drive in.

Welcoming the others and shake hands with Tom, Fed went into his cart and fell asleep next to Dan.

In the fort, some of the people were busy collecting the dead on a barrow. Another part of the men started digging a big pit. And the women, instructing the big children to take care of the little ones outside, prepared a few sleeping places. Then they gathered everything edible and prepared it together. By evening the grave had been closed and rocked. Everyone gathered around it. The guide prayed, then they observed a few minute's of silence and went out for dinner. After they agreed to sleep at the fort and to have a meeting.

Around 8 pm the meeting was opened and Tom was the first to speak.

"You have chosen me to lead this meeting as your trek leader. Thanks! First of all, I would like to say that all of present are of 21 years of age. I have gathered all the concerns and read them right away. I'll answer a question that I've been asked a lot before.

Yeah, I'm staying, but only two months, and I'll tell you what we have to reach till then. Now to the agenda of the meeting. First of all, who should continue to be 'in charge'.

Secondly, what needs to be done in terms of construction and cultivation.

Thirdly, the development of a school and legislative plan.

Fourth plan on...

During the meeting, Dan went through the house systematically, by his way. The central point was, a so-called middle room in which everything took place during the day. Of course, this had to be examined first.

Dan is as already mentioned 8 years, emaciated from the exertions of the journey,

a thin white linen shirt and blue trousers
dresses him. He has straight, light blond hair,
star-blue eyes and sun-tanned skin.
As a precaution, he's got a knife in his hand
that he traded from Tom with irresistible
child - looking eyes. A custom-made path
knife.
Dan could have held it with three hands. It
was so long that when he put it in the side of
his snake leather belt that his father made
him, it tapped him with the tip to his knee
while running.
The knife firmly raised, jerking the corners,
Dan paced through the house. Since nothing
of the things had been cleared out yet, he
thought nothing had been looked through yet.
For these reasons he put all his expedition
treasures on the table in the middle room.
It became a chaotic heap from silver cutlery
to a botanical collection with maps of the
area.
After he had looked through everything, it
looked like a hurricane went through, on the
table and all around.
When he tried to sort the whole thing, he fell
asleep.
When the parents came home, they were
slightly frightened until they saw Dan
sleeping in the pile. So they had to be careful
not to wake him up by laughing.
"I'll put him to bed first," said his mother.
When they came back, they locked each
other and the chaos. Started laughing again.

"Now he knows everything we have." Fed.
"Yeah, more than me and I already had a lot sorted in a certain place.- But I didn't know the maps and plant boxes here." Jenny
"In this case, he's ahead of us. But to be smarter then, he can help you clean up tomorrow." Fed.
"He'll be glad." Jenny
"Nothing can help him to escape." Fed.
Suddenly Tom comes in and looks at Fed and Jenny, Dan's mother, and burst out laughing.
"Ah, here some one has made you trouble, job, Jenny," says Tom.
Since Jenny did not answer right away, Fed said with a slight smile, "Dan is more thorough than we are, nothing remains unexamined.
Actually, I'm proud that Dan is so bright and well inquisitive. We're just scared here in the wild. It's certainly not appropriate."
"I'll give you the advice to teach Dan early how to shoot. On his first trip, he should be able to. Stopping it would be wrong "that'll break Dan for sure.
I'll take him as long as I'm here, if you don't mind." Tom suggested.
"No, it would certainly be the best," said the father.
"If there really is no other way, teach him everything, and if it takes longer, I beg you, I'm afraid something will happen to Dan." Fed.
-

" I'll take him to the gunsmith tomorrow to measure," Tom said, "then we'll see."

With the arrangement they went, smiling once more to the pile, then to sleep.

The next morning Tom went with Dan, after he had heard of his clean-up fate, from his father, early to the gunsmith's shop, who was already equipping himself to offer something else.

"Hello Tom, what can I do for you," he asked immediately putting down a box and sitting on it.

"I need a rifle..." Tom.

Without letting Tom say, "Yours was so good, isn't there anything more you can do?"

"I want it for Fed's son, I brought him to measure." Tom.

"Well, come on Dan, it's not my money that goes out through the window, I'm just picking it up." The blacksmith said

After a while they came back to the shop section.

"What should your wish look like in particular, he will fall if he just touches the tap."

"That is your job, it should sit comfortable in his hand, shoot like any rifle, you only have to reduce the recoil." Tom.

"You have nerves you know exactly that the clout is about to wane", Blacksmith.

"When can I pick it up? 3 days are enough for you. " Tom.

"Tom."

He didn't answer any more and was already leaving.

"Then at least send the boy over to me every morning." Smith.

"That's OK," came from afar.

"Why do you do that?"asked Dan - Tom.

"To ensure the safety of your life." Tom.

"Nobody does anything to me." Dan.

"Not here, but can you promise to stay in the fort forever?" Tom asked, glancing at Dan from the side.

They were silent the rest of the way.

It was only in front of the house that Dan said, "But I can't shoot at all and what if the recoil is really too big?"

"Then we have to see that we can deal with it. Now go in, we both still have something to do. " Tom.

"Yes Sir," replied Dan and went inside. He didn't like tidying up at all, but he did understand it.

The construction turmoil had already begun in the fort. The noise of saws and hammers filled the air. Instructions were shouted through the air, which when carried out and led to a really satisfied result. They used what was already there and tried to redesign it according to their taste according to all the rules of art and craftsmanship.

In the evening the men examined with the women and children what they had not cleaned up during the day. Mainly there were things that were already in the house, but not part of everyday use. For example the botanist collection. Finally, the children were already asleep and an agreement was reached on the whereabouts of the men's work materials.

For many this was also new, many were also sons of lords or fathers who had a job that was of no use to them here and wanted to try their chances as farmers on the promised land.

In the next few days, the work went on easier and they got used to it. Sometimes the children were scolded if they got too close to where the building was going.

Dan, on the other hand, learned to read traces from Tom and, through the luck of having a botanical collection, got to know some poisonous and some edible plants. In addition, 3 plants whose sap is good for wounds, which he himself learned from the "blacks".

Since Dan spent the whole day with Tom, he first took up the task of expanding his tasks in combination with other things, letting him read the names from the collection himself and the explanation of the dead botanist.

He was just wondering what he wrote about the plants and had Dan write down the text on one plant every day.

In the meantime they went to pick up the rifle. It was a >> lady's rifle << that was shortened once more and was padded with cotton and metal spring sheet on the back.

In this way, the kickback should be absorbed by at least to a half.

Now Dan also learned to shoot, first of all he went down and everyone laughed.

If Tom hadn't held him, he would have had run away.

"Let me, he said it right away already," shouted Dan at him and wanted to free himself. But the hands that held him were like screw clamps. The hands of a hunter, those of the guide, held him like a merciless trap. It wasn't until Dan calmed down again that Tom said, "You can't stand stiffly, straight like a board behind it. You are not a tree, you can be moved. Be glad a tree that bothers some one is simply felled, or are there several just pathetically burned or blown up. A hunter needs the trees as protection from the weather, rain or other - or support.

In some trees you can also find certain animals and if you have read the botanist's texts correctly, you will know that some plants can also be found predominantly on certain trees. So think twice about cutting down a tree, otherwise you will soon find nothing at all.

Check it out in the fort, just sand.

But now come so you can learn how to shoot, I'll help you. " Tom.

So he showed him how to stand and shoot at standing objects.

Over time, these increased in distance and decreased in size.

Tom got him to the point that Dan also managed a so-called blind shooting.

It looked like that the bottles with threads were hung up until the thread could no longer be seen. Dan should >> calculate << on the slope where the thread is and then shoot it through.

Later they were rocking and flying, then rolling, ending with several movements.

For this purpose Tom had built strips of bushes, twigs, which he could change in a flash with different strings of thread.

Doses were rolled onto it, which Dan should shoot at the same moment if Tom wanted to. In order to increase the reaction speed, and to train for the startle reaction, cans were thrown at him directly from the front, or from behind in some direction, which he should then hit.

So that Dan didn't get trigger-happy, the distance between the shooting practice was extended from time to time so that he wouldn't shoot anything that was moving. In the meantime, Dan had learned other things as well.

Now he also knew how to pack the back-bag in a certain order, including his bags and the reason why what should be packed when. Or how to build a safe shelter, determine the direction and determine the weather in advance through the animals. In addition, how to break open his prey, that is, how to remove the organs.

He learned to make a campfire, to prepare something to eat from it, to make useful things from the skin of the animals and to keep the fire at a certain height. They both sewed a Back-bag and new clothes for him, but Jenny also sewed with them.

A year had passed and Tom would have liked to have been gone a long time, but he wasn't a man who started something and didn't finish it. Besides, he didn't let anyone down and on the other hand, he also enjoyed it, because Dan was a good student. Dan didn't bother reading and writing either because the readings were interesting. So the very much reduced playing time didn't bother him.

In the evening he still walked and ran a little because Tom said that someone in the jungle often had to walk for days and sometimes very quickly. If he could not shoot then, he would run in vain.

The first days in the jungle

In the evening Tom was still sitting outside on the stairs in front of the door.

Since it was long past midnight, Fed went out, he knew that Tom would only do something like this if he had something important to do for him the next day. Fed sat quietly next to him and took in the evening air with relish.

For a long time they sat there in silence, as if they both suspected something and watched the last memories like a film covered with a veil.

"I've been expecting you," said Tom, breaking the silence.

But there was only silence following.

Fed had let himself be carried away by the silence, heard the sentence but did not answer it.

"You entrusted your son to me, I'll take him with me," Tom broke the silence for good.

Fed just asked "when?"

"With the sun is coming up ?" Tom.

"Does Dan know"? Fed.

"No, - he should sleep peacefully, I sent him early and let him run really tired before. So that he sleeps. " Tom.

"And Jenny ?" Fed.

"No, I knew you were coming." Tom.

There was another short silence.

"How is he doing except when shooting, we've all seen that." Fed.

"Well, he's a very good student, you can leave him alone soon. - If I had a son like that, I would be proud of him, I did love to be his teacher. " Tom.

"He also had a good teacher." Fed.

"He still has." Tom.

The silence continued.

When the nautical twilight began, so the sky began to turn red, Tom got up, touched Fed by the shoulder and said, "Let's go wake Jenny and Dan. Jenny should see Dan again before. "

So they went in.

When the four of them, Dan and Tom, stood in front of the fort and hugged each other goodbye, Jenny cried, partly because she was happy that Dan was finally ready, on the other hand she didn't know whether they would see each other again. Tom was a good hunter, but even for him there could be something to big for him, to danger in the jungle.

Tom went easy with Dan, he planned up to 2 days without chasing a target or anything special. He wanted Dan to shoot something that would be enough for both of them that evening and the next day.

But in the first time Dan was so overwhelmed by joy and excitement that he wanted to hunt everything right away. But Tom said he only wanted a small animal, a very specific one.

Then Dan calmed down, he had heard from many hunters, which had been on the road for days and weeks just to hunt a tiger, a rhinoceros or something similar and thought that something so important also had to be hunted.

Tom noticed the calm and began to show him some animals and explained their habits so that Dan wouldn't raise his rifle because of the noise. Dan also got to know the plants from the collection in nature and told Tom what he had kept in mind about them. By copying it, he had memorized and processed the explanation very well. He also learned from the botanist's books. Tom used the boy's whole curiosity.

At lunchtime they did not stop, but ate on the way from the supplies they had taken with them.

In the afternoon Tom knelt, waiting for Dan's reaction.

But Dan noticed it right away and went down on his knees in a flash without a sound.

Looked around, he hadn't heard anything special, but he noticed that Tom was only looking at the floor.

"Well, heart in your pocket?" asked Tom with a smile.

"No, not really," he said, embarrassed, but then laughed.

"Come, I'll show you something" and pointed to a trail, clearing a little grass for it.

"A gazelle" shouted Dan immediately, so that the birds in the tree that stood a little further away, fled.

"Yes, but what does that mean?" Tom.

"She is sick or got lost." Dan.

"And?" Tom.

"That tigers or lions or something will come soon." Dan.

"Yes, what are your legs saying." Tom.

"Are OK, why?" Dan.

"Then let's try to be there before the others." Tom.

So they went on at a quiet run, checking the track from time to time.

Tom took Dan's backpack so he could walk easily and comfortably. They had to run for quite a while, so Tom was afraid that Dan wouldn't be able to make it through. But at the last moment they saw the gazelle. Stopping Dan carefully, he gave him signs from where to stalk. Because of the wind. But suddenly the wind turned and the gazelle picked up the scent. "Shoot" shouted Tom, taking his rifle at the ready to hit it if necessary. But it wasn't necessary, noticing the change in behaviour, Dan shot as if on command during the exercises from the past. The gazelle collapsed with the first shot. In order to steer Dan's reaction, Tom tried to drag him along for hunting luck.

But then they cut out a large piece, cleaned it, and wrapped it up.

Then they set out to get enough distance from the prey to not attract other hunting animals to them.

"Wait a minute, we're going to repack the meat," said Tom after they had walked for a while. "Wrap the cloth in between, it has a plant scent, so we don't attract predators if they smell the meat. And let's find a camp now. -

Would you like to sleep upstairs or downstairs. "

"What you mean upstairs?" Dan.

"On a tree." Tom.

"But the fire, how do we do that with the fire?" asked Dan.

"We'll do that upstairs, the guard will keep it up." Tom.

"Okay, let's find a nice tree." Dan.

"And wood," called Tom after the bright boy. Actually he had said this just for fun, now he had to cope with it, because he didn't want to disappoint him either.

Suddenly a shot rang out that made Tom, who was trotting behind, startled and run. Immediately it shot through his head, 'A lion or some other animal, he can't handle. I Shouldn't have let him run alone if something happened to him now. No, that may not be'. But then he heard a laugh, he looked around and saw Dan climbing up a tree.

Since Tom noticed that Dan hadn't seen him yet, he hid and let him be a child again before he wanted to call him back to reality.

When he watched him climb, he wished he'd like to be a little child again.

Tom had to be careful not to lose his vigilance.

After a while he called out, "Dan did you have to shoot right away, cartridges are precious and you scared me a lot."

"Sorry, but you said that if there are several people on the way and something is found, that's how you communicate." Dan apologized, his head bowed.

"Fine. - Come, we have to stretch the tent covers in the branches. You go up, I'll throw it up for you, but hold on tight. " Tom.

"OK, my things are already up there." Dan.

"How did you do that?' Tom.

"With the rope ..." Dan.

"Yea okay," said Tom, "I really could have thought of that too".

They stretched Dan's canvas and then pulled Tom's luggage afterwards, and then finally stretched his canvas as well. Then they went down to make a fire.

After they took the meat skewering it on a peeled branch and hung it over the fire on a branch - fork.

"How did you like it today," Tom said.

"Just great, we didn't see so many animals on arrival." Dan.

"But now we also have to divide up the night watch." Tom.

"And if I can't stay awake." Dan.

"That's the problem, you have to hold on. We have practised it now show what you can do. - he said it with a smile - you start and when you notice, it no longer works, you tell me. But that has to work." Tom.

"o.k." Dan.

"Just OK, well." Tom.

Then they ate and dried the rest of the meat. When Dan had been awake for 3 hours, he could no longer keep himself awake and woke Tom, who was a light sleeper.

In the meantime Dan had packed his backpack several times and saved space, but that no longer kept him awake. Not even carving a piece of wood.

Tom took over the rest of the watch for till two hours left. It was already light but he wanted to lie down again and told Dan to wake him up. Everything except for the blankets should be packed so that they can leave straight away.

Since this was an animal water path, Dan saw many animals again, some of which he did not yet know.

In his imagination he imagined riding a giraffe in England, against horses, of course he won too.

But then everyone shook their heads and didn't give him the prize. Nevertheless, everyone wanted a giraffe at once and he could no longer save himself from the fine girls, Dan would of course have won for them.

But as there where more and more girls coming, it got too much for Dan and he woke up from his imagination.

He looked at Tom's watch and swallowed, it was a quarter of an hour later. He knew that Tom wouldn't say anything, but he wasn't quite comfortable. He hadn't really paid attention. When Tom woke up, he noticed that something was wrong, but said nothing.

"Will you pack the blankets, please, I want to freshen up a little." Tom.

"OK, OK" Dan.

"You already have a good vocabulary, can you say a bit more than, OK.?" Tom.

Now they both had to laugh, now Tom said OK too.

When Tom came back everything was already packed and they could leave.

On the way everyone told something about themselves. Tom had a lot to tell, he had been in the jungle for over 20 years, he also told a lot of hunter fairy tales.

But Dan was more cautious and no longer believed everything. Tom told him of a zombie tiger whose mind couldn't calm down because he was simply shot from behind while trying to escape. Now, he said, "whoever kills an animal unnecessarily or takes more meat with him than he needs and spoils it, the tiger will come for him."

Dan didn't really feel at ease with it, but only Tom himself seemed to believe it. He wondered that an adult could believe that. But Tom seemed visibly afraid of it.

Since there was silence afterwards, Dan tried to ask him about the animals he did not know and had seen that morning. It was very difficult because Tom was attuned to a different topic.

In the evening Tom looked sadly at the sun and thought - 'Well we won't make it today, I hope they don't worry too much.' So he asked

Dan if he was tired. Dan knew Tom very well by now and knew what he meant by that.
He just asked, "How much is it then?"
"The sun will be down for two hours." Tom.
"We can walk, it's okay." Dan.
Then they had to laugh again, OK. was just Dan's catchphrase.
"Can we take something for home," Dan asked shyly, knowing that they had no more time. Surprisingly and to Dan's delight, Tom said, "The next bird that arises is yours, to take us lunch for tomorrow."
Now Dan was paying twice as much attention, he didn't want to miss the first bird. The first thing that flew by was a vulture, but nobody wanted h i m.
The second bird to rise was a stork. Dan reacted in a split second that amazed even Tom.
Hit by the first shot, the stork fell to the ground.
"What is he doing here," asked Dan, surprised.
"Don't you know the storks come to Africa when it gets too cold in Europe. - Now it should be Christmas soon in England. " Tom.
"Yes, and here you sweat yourself ready for a bathe, and then you have to be careful not to accidentally cover the nose from a crocodile with you feet." Dan.
They both had to laugh a lot. "You don't have a bad sense of humor, i have to give that to you," replied Tom.

Since there were no more beautiful birds to be found, they shot another kudu, a species of a antelope.

So they had a great burden, that they had to take a break.

They arrived at the fort around 10 o'clock in the evening, but Tom was happy, he had now expected even later.

In the fort they were announced from the tower.

That had the consequence that everyone was on its feet and if they just wanted to see how the boy had held out, or simply not to be absent. The children greeted him almost as he imagined in his giraffe race. To prevent this and out of tiredness, Dan disappeared voluntarily in a flash speed.

Tom brought the antelope into the house and talked to the parents.

The gunsmith came later and swapped a now empty whiskey bottle for a full one, with the assurance that it was a really Scottish one.

"My rifle was good, wasn't it" said the gunsmith.

Tom immediately replied, "would I have bought it otherwise?"

"No, I really don't think so." Blacksmith

They talked for a long time, also about Dan and what might become of him.

The next morning Dan was very excited, he had to cut his own shot animal into pieces, since they had never been able to eat the whole thing at once and the fur had to be removed. Dan wanted to do all the work on his own, but since he couldn't do it, he ended up hitching everyone up.

After all the work was done, Dan eagerly went on telling the children about the adventures.

He wonders what horror stories have already spread.

He just told himself if he had experienced it the way it was told, he would have been scared and not closed his eyes while sleeping.

Even so, he didn't say much, because the nonsense made him more respected, but kept the truth in his stories and only that.

Dan went on many safaris with Tom.

The hunt for an injured lion

One morning there was unrest in the fort. A farmer had met a lion outside but fatally hit him without striking him down, now he was unpredictable.

Since Tom had not yet finished his apprenticeship with Dan, he was still in the camp and asked for advice and guidance.

"Good, I'm in. get your backpacks ready and bring plenty of ammunition and a net. We run...."

They interrupted him, "you want to run are you insane."

"We can't get through everywhere with the horses and I only take with those who can shoot properly.

I don't want to ask the lions after a missed shot how much try's I still have left. " Tom. Then he went back inside.

"Dan pack your things, now we're doing something like a preliminary test," Tom called to him, who reacted immediately.

"Do you really want to take him there," asked Fed.

"Yes, it is the penultimate time that I go with him. I heard that another ship has arrived, so I'll take him with me for the last time. He's been following me for six months and already knows the area for several thousand miles and can already guide me, he doesn't get any better. With a map from the botanists who were with you, he can get along in areas where I haven't even been till with him. Can you tell me what else to show Dan now? " Tom.

'I'll join you.' Fed.

"I honestly didn't expect it any different." Tom.

So they packed their bags and Jenny said goodbye to all three with tears.

She had got used to it with Dan for a while, but an unpredictable lion was too much for her.

Outside, the others said that Dan should just slow them down and should stay.

"He's never slowed me down, he's coming with me. Better tell me where our "master marksman" is, we have to know the place where he lost the lion. He should show Dan the place on the map, he knows his way around better than me. " Tom.

There were 10 men and Dan, they were all good shooters, except the one who wanted to shoot the lion.

They had to walk for three hours before they found the trail.

"Dan what do you think of that," asked Tom.

"Won't be fast, but the bounce is still there. The bulled will lie in such a way that the right paw can almost no longer be used, " answered the questioned.

"How does he want to know all this?" Asked one of the crowd.

"Because he learned from me, I wouldn't say anything else here," Tom replied angrily.

They followed the trail and Tom let Dan lead little by little.

He felt satisfied, now he had taught Dan everything he knew about the jungle and the steppe. Yes, Dan had even gotten a little better, he had learned everything from the botanists.

The experiences, were years of experience he didn't have and he was proud that Dan learned it so well.

Tom came tears even at the thought and watching.

He later spoke to Fed about Dan.

"Well, do you see it now? we can leave Dan alone, he won't go under, more like one of those >> hot-tempered << boys there, "said Tom.

"Yes you are right, thank you. Now I can be sure and sleep more peacefully if he should "move out". Fed.

"Something will come of him again, he will help a lot of people and show them where to go. Maybe the Queen will listen to him one day. - I would like to get a seat later from where I can see your son's fame. " Tom.

"That sounds like, you will see it." Fed.

It was evening and camp was set up, guards were assigned and the others went to sleep. So 3 days and nights went by without anything happening. The others wondered if he still had the trace. They asked Tom what was going on, if they wouldn't find him soon, he shouldn't be that fare. Tom only said that he had only followed the trail until yesterday but then relied on Dan. Then they went to Dan and asked him to admit that he had lost the trail without asking any further questions. Suddenly there was a bang, Tom shot into the air.

"Why don't you try to ask him what's going on, person to person." Tom.

Then one of the crowd said, "He should show us the trail."

Dan said, "You wouldn't believe that either. You wouldn't be sure if it's the same, if you don't believe me, you don't have to keep going. "

But since nobody knew exactly where they were, they were forced to follow. But they realized that they had to rely on Dan.

It was noticeable that this time the teacher followed the student.

On the morning of the fourth day, Dan was gone.

Tom angrily asked who was on guard, it came out that it was the "master marksman", as he was called after his mishap. Fed wanted to go to his throat right away and insulted him all the time. Tom took his jacket and lifted him slightly.

"Remember one thing, I ate you."

After saying this, he just let him fall.

But when they had collected themselves and calmed down and wanted to decide how to proceed because there was no trace of him to be found, Dan appeared and asked him angrily. "Is that the bullet", and held one out to the "championship shooter".

The gunsmith who came with them confirmed it.

"Dilettante," said Dan, putting the ball in a neck pouch and walking on.

Nobody said anything that the boy might have overstated or anything. The argument was also forgotten, everyone prepared to leave without anyone saying anything. After an hour they started to return.

No one said anything all day. It was only when they set up a camp again towards the evening they became more relaxed. Then it turned out that the lion was too far away and has been shot from behind, but what happened next was that he had slept and hadn't even noticed a snake. With that he could never notice Dan's departure.

It was agreed that it should be made out in the fort according to the established laws. That same evening, their camp, became attacked by a pack of hyena dogs. It took them half the night to defend themselves. But only the marksman was injured because he couldn't shoot properly.

But since they all needed sleep, it was decided to leave later and only tended to the wounds.

When the sun was almost half past on zenith, they set out. Nothing happened for the rest of the day, it was only when they were only a day's journey away from the fort that the marksman had a high fever in the morning and could not get up. He hadn't changed the bandage.

They gave him English medicine that they had bought a few months ago so he got a chance. They made a stretcher out of tent cloth and branches and took turns carrying him. From then on, a hyena accompanied them at a distance, you only heard her now and then, and therefore they knew that she was there. Vultures soon joined them. The one on the stretcher began to fanatical.

He died shortly before they entered the fort. This time the joy of coming home was a little clouded.

It was decided that everyone except Dan, because of his age, from the group to where the funeral was going to be held, would keep wake with him in the church until morning. Dan didn't want to be mutually exclusive, but he was still not allowed to participate.

The next morning he was buried in the same place as the others who were in the fort before them.

A new trek

Hardly two days had passed when Tom and Dan prepared to leave again. On that day the whole fort helped with the preparations, as new people from Europe were supposed to arrive at the fort, led by the two of them.

The people had now realized that Dan had really learned enough to survive alone in the jungle and the steppes.

The next day they left at dawn. Tom liked to go at such a time. He then found it still quite pleasantly cool.

Dan it was not important when they set off, the main thing was - he was on the way and could experience a lot.

They had ridden for three days, well into the night, until they rested more. They put up their tents and planned the further course and route of the trip. To do this, they spread a blanket and checked the supplies.

"We'll have to include hunting soon, supplies will run out soon," said Tom.

"How long will it take us?" Asked Dan.

"We'll still need four to five days." Tom.

"But it took us a good two weeks." Dan.
"Yes, but without much hunting, just with provisions. We might be faster without horses, mobility is simply the most important thing here. " Tom.
They talked until late at night before they went to sleep, they had secured the camp well in a wide area so that they would have heard an animal intruding in time.
After four days they arrived at the port, where the new ones were already waiting.
"Well today with an attachment", asked a salesman who had known Tom for a long time, "
Tom. "Yes, he was once my student, but now he has everything I can teach him."
"And we already thought it got you." seller
"Well now you have a replacement." Tom.
"Don't tell such nonsense." Seller
"No, he's already been on a safari." Tom.
"I don't mean that, you know that. But you still have to tell me more about the safari. " Seller
He took out a bottle of whiskey and they sat down. Tom said he just let Dan lead and didn't bother about it later. They both laughed then he asked.
"Didn't they look surprised when they noticed?" his friend asked.
Of course. Tom then told him all. They often laughed in between.
"That would have been an experience for me too, believe me." Seller

"They wouldn't even have been able to manage an antelope that lives here and would have to rely on her." Tom.

While laughing, said the seller, "she would have been very surprised about her new children."

Now they couldn't hold back from laughing and Tom almost dropped the glass. Still laughing, the salesman said, "I like to picture it in front of a handful of hunters on all fours behind an antelope and roaring, calling Mama."

Taking a deep breath, he continued calmly. "But the antelope turns around, sniffs, counts, and then waves a leg to follow."

Now the last was over and they laughed through tears for a very long time.

When they calmed down they exchanged the latest news and by the time they headed to bed it was a long time since Tom and Dan arrived.

The next day, under some demonstrations, Tom and Dan explained what they needed to know first for the beginning. Then they started to buy the essentials.

In the afternoon Tom announced the departure, early in the morning at sunrise.

The next day, a small troop set out, again a few people who moved from their homeland to seek a new life elsewhere.

The first day was difficult, they made little progress, the heat and the walk and driving caused them great initial difficulties.

Towards evening they set up a camp and guards including his self a turn to guard.

Not much happened in the next few days. In the evenings, Tom and Dan always discussed the new route for the next day and usually found that they had gotten a little faster, but still too slow.

"I don't understand so few people this time but it's the slowest I've ever had.

They're having a hard time adjusting, and there are almost no children with them," Tom said to Dan.

"Who knows how they're going to get along in the settlement. I talked to them once, nobody really has a clue about anything." Dan.

"Well, that will show." Tom.

This time they had discussed the final route to the fort and there was no word from Tom that Dan should go to sleep. This worried Dan, he had a bad feeling, but he stayed seated until they left.

The next day, Dan didn't even feel tired, only the uneasy feeling remained.

They got ready to march and set off after the route was announced.

Around noon clouds of smoke could be seen in the distance and the sound of drums gradually drowned out the usual sounds of Africa.

"It can either be for us, or for two tribes who have different opinions of each other."

Tom ended up trying to be a little funny to sound like a bit funny.

But Dan, with whom he talked almost inclusively, unless there was something important for the others, knew what to expect.

They tried to get to an open field, with the possibility of forming a wagon train at any time.

When the two picked up their guns, no sign was needed this time, it went like an echo, or rather a chain reaction, of falling dominoes standing close together.

"Hopefully they'll react faster when it comes to the wagons," both said almost simultaneously.

"Dan you ride to the middle to make it go fast," Tom finally said.

"No, I want to stay with you, you need me up here." Dan.

Dan cried lightly, thinking of the night that looked like goodbyes. He knew that Tom sensed it beforehand when something was about to happen and he also remembered the parting words before they left the fort. Dan never wanted to believe that a European could develop such a feeling. But if you've been busy living in nature long enough, observing it, hearing it and feeling with it... He too knew that he was about to lose a friend, because he now believed in the omens.

"It's time, please," Tom interrupted his thoughts. They both looked deep into each other's eyes again, then they shook hands. Just before Dan was about to drop to the middle, Tom said, "Don't worry, we'll see each other again".

Dan wasn't long behind when a few warriors appeared out of the grass throwing spears and then disappeared again, replaced by new warriors.

It seemed as if there were more and more. Panic broke out among the people and the two had a hard time forcing them to form a group of wagons. when they finally had a group of wagons and the first warriors fell without being able to do anything, it became quiet. Even the animals couldn't be heard, which was an ominous sign. Vultures were the only ones quick to show up, quietly awaiting their meal. After one round, Tom found that there were injuries, but nothing serious.

"What do we do now?" they asked Tom.

But he didn't say anything, just watched the grass. To tell the people something, Dan said. We are waiting.

"Let's wait until they come back and kill us all, we have to get away." said one of the crowd who was the blacksmith and many grumbled.

Even Tom hadn't expected this nonsensical reaction.

"And what do you do when we're back in line and they come back. Next time they'll definitely hit it better, because we're not going there yet, because then they'll choose the best point. Since we're all very busy then," replied Tom, calmly controlling himself.

It didn't take long either, as they also reappeared, like last time, out of nowhere. In which then all seemed to disappear again. But this time they shot small arrows and also threw burning >>torches<<.

Dan and Tom both wondered because they had never seen this tribe before. The ones with their arrows were very fast and therefore very seldom disappearing. However, these did not seem to belong to them directly.

Since many warriors fell and they were horrified to discover that the leather shields offered no protection, silence fell again and they disappeared.

Meanwhile, everyone tried to repair the damage done and smother the fires.

In this attack there were dead, a woman and a boy were hit by arrows.

"How long is this supposed to last or can we finally move on?" asked the blacksmith, who was now trying to gain the upper hand by agitating and talking.

"Maybe until all of us are dead or they realize we're stronger, if that's true. I don't see that until now," Tom replied.

"What do you mean, does that mean it's over anyway and it doesn't matter where we die?" the blacksmith asked him.

"That's what it means if you stir up more trouble and they don't all react quicker soon. Also, it's about time everyone started doing what we say, but so does everyone," Dan said, with a little wicked undertone since he was starting to dislike him a little.

"You are silent when adults are talking. Do we have to listen to that from a brat, he's really cheeky," said the blacksmith again.

Now furious, Tom stood in front of the blacksmith with all his might. It looked ridiculous, the blacksmith, who was strong and tall because of his trade, seemed quite small and weak, he only reached Tom's shoulders. then he took a deep breath and said, "That boy, my friend, is very right. Dan knows more about this area than any of you and in case you haven't figured it out, you all depend on him. So I hope that in the future you will all listen to what he says if you want to survive here in the wilderness. Just so you know, they're not the first to arrive sane at the fort under his leadership, if you listen to him. Nothing has happened to anyone because of him.

Now it is your turn".

But the blacksmith said nothing more, but was visibly dissatisfied.

Nothing happened until the evening, only the drums sounded again and crushed the last nerves of the people. But in the evening the lawn suddenly started to burn.

"Great, they've come up with something great and now," asked the blacksmith, "now it's really over, we had to sit around here too."

"We don't have to, we join in," Dan said.

"What's that supposed to mean again, hey guide, what the devil does he mean now?"

"Please leave him out of the game, that would be better. But I don't know what he means this time either, I think he'll tell us," replied Tom the blacksmith.

The others skeptically, under Dan's direction, gathered thick logs which they piled in a meter around the castle behind, they burned piece by piece a strip a width of 2 meters at a distance of one meter from the >wall<. When they finished, the fire was only 2 meters from the wall. And Dan let these burn, they burned in all places almost at the same time.

The fire spread quickly on the narrow strip, so that both fire fronts collided and there was nothing more flammable and it finally went out.

In the end, Tom was amazed too, it seemed logical that if nothing flammable was left, it couldn't burn anymore. But no one believed that they would come up with it and start something like that.

Stimulated by the silence and imagination, Dan whispered something in a girl's ear that suddenly made them laugh out loud. Furious, suspecting they might laugh at him, the smith asked, "Why are you laughing?"

Dan immediately replied with a laugh, "I imagined that they had put so much effort into the fire and maybe they even summoned the spirits for it. Now they will think our fire is even stronger than theirs. They've also broken their own cover."

Everyone started laughing and the blacksmith couldn't remember whether they were laughing at him or at Dan's joke. Just one thing everyone knew, Dan wasn't making fun of the warriors, just laughing at his childish imagination.

They knew Dan respected the natives and might get along with them, which nobody hoped for.

Shortly before sunrise the next offensive began, they too had realized that they had destroyed their only surprise cover. Of course with the hope of destroying their opponent with it. But now they came running in their hundreds and shot as much as they could with the same material as the day before.

This time more was destroyed and hit, Dan got a mirror from the barber to hide behind and waited by shooting at those who were about to shoot without killing them.

At last the sun rose and soon shone with sufficient force.

Now Dan stood behind the mirror on one of the wagons and held the mirror so that it blinded the warriors.

At first they looked at each other in horror, everyone shimmered reddish. As the sun got brighter, they too were blinded more and more and it got hotter too. Both sides stood shocked.

When Dan noticed that the mirror was developing heat, he took another small one out of his pocket and focused it on a warrior's arrows until they started to burn.

It looked like Dan was setting the arrows on fire with a glowing hand. This became too much of an incomprehensible miracle for the warriors, they dropped everything and fled. Relieved, they tended to the wounded and repaired the wagons.

Suddenly the girl ran towards Dan with tears in her eyes, but since she couldn't get a word out, Dan came with her. As he stood in the car he was startled, there lay Tom he had been hit in the lungs by an arrow just next to the heart.

Dan got the memories of the farewell and he started to cry.

Tom noticed him right away and said, "I knew you were going to get us out of here. You didn't get your name for nothing from your parents without knowing it. Do you know what this name means?"

Dan shook his head because he couldn't say anything now, realizing that he was alone with Tom and sat down next to him. You should! Your name is derived from Daniel, you know the name from the Bible and it is

Hebrew, dãnijje'l and means my judge is God. That's why you also try that there is no way to judge and in return you have all the skill. Believe me, I've been looking for an explanation for a long time because I was interested in the strength and friendship that radiates. I am proud of you and filled with great joy to have had you as a student. The last years with you and your parents were the best of my life. Come help me to remember a little.

Remember how you told me about the dream about the giraffe race and we tried to catch a little one." Tom.

"Yes, we were so knocked out that we could hardly walk anymore. But when we managed to surprise one, we couldn't even hold on to her a little bit. We put ourselves on the ground there." Dan.

"Yes." Tom.

They both smiled a little, but Dan immediately cried again. It played like a movie before their eyes again. Tom started again, "remember how we ran from a rhino because you were so desperate to keep it alive and when we realized we couldn't make it to the next tree. Then you suddenly turned around and yelled at it. >Go away.<

"Yeah, it was so shocked it actually took off." Dan.

"Yes, that was really a good time with you and so exciting and funny even for me. But tell me what did you do with the lion we were hunting. When you ran off in the night and scared us real bad?" Tom.

Dan had a hard time telling it when he was crying, but he did it anyway.

"I shot him with an anaesthetic poison, removed the bullet, put some of your medicinal herbs in and gummed it up. That'll come off later." Dan.

"Yes, actually I wanted you to be my successor later, but I know it won't work. You'll do more, but that makes me even happier. You have made me the happiest man and you make your parents the richest people in the world. But now you have to promise me one thing. Lead the people into the fort and then keep learning. You see now the tiger has me too - he doesn't even have to come himself. I brought too many people here who only destroy, who are now also on me, that was my fault. God said when he gave us the earth, conquer the earth. But what are we going to do, we're about to destroy her, the only thing left to do is pray that people will stop soon enough, when she still has the strength to recover without destroying us. Because it's like the flu, either the person and the flu come along because there are no more nutrients. Or people develop antibodies and the flu breaks down. On earth we are the flu. Remember that." Tom.

Then he closed his eyes and was dead. Dan wasn't crying anymore, although he was sad that he had now lost a great friend, but he was also glad that Tom was happy about his last years.

He picked up some things Tom had once promised him and then walked out of the car. There the girl's mother was waiting for him and said, "I'll get him ready for the funeral."

"Thanks." Dan.

Dan also had the warriors buried just like he had seen a tribe do from afar. But he prayed in front of everyone, which made some hate him. For them, the << blacks>> simply had to rot in the open or be eaten by the animals. At Tom's grave he stayed alone for a while until finally the girl's mother picked him up. "I don't understand you, but you'll stay with us until the fort, at least then you'll be accepted as you are. Come on."

Arriving at the wagons, the others argued about who should take them further. Part of it was that Tom had said they needed Dan to guide them before, which the blacksmith didn't like, nor did his followers. Others felt that the teacher who was with them should lead them, which he didn't want to do because he knew he couldn't do it one iota like Dan.

"What are you arguing about, does anyone have any idea where to go?" Dan asked to the arguing crowd.

"No, but you have cards, give them to us and then we'll be fine," said the smith.

"Yes, give us the cards," shouted one of the crowd.

"And when you have the maps you know where you are and in which direction you have to go, I don't have a compass."
Again the blacksmith said with the agreement of many, "if you show us where we are and once the direction then it will be fine."
"I'm sorry, I only have everything in my head, I just know my home." Dan.
"You can't get away from us that cheaply, search his pockets," yelled the blacksmith, not wanting to give up. then the mother fired a shot, "don't you believe anything anymore, its enough. The next is the one who even touches something from him."
"Never mind, it's okay, they won't find anything," Dan replied, gently pushing the gun down of her. But no one did anything, they all went quietly to their car.
"Now you've won, but I'll wait and then I'll crush you," said the blacksmith and left.
"You ride with us in the car, we'll just drive in front," said the woman.
"But I'll take the teacher as an intermediary, he's still well under control," Dan said, speaking to him.
"You just have to make sure that everyone stays together and report any disruptive incident to the front to me. I know it's not that easy, but I just want you, you can do it." Dan said to the teacher.
After an hour they moved on and by the sound of the drums again they knew they were being watched.

"What are the drums saying, my mom tells me, the drums are always saying something," asked the girl.

Her name was Nadiene and she was a little girl of eight, with brown eyes and black hair and with her snub nose she looked more like a doll with a pigtail who moved and asked a lot of questions.

She wore a light blue dress, which didn't stay very light anymore due to the trip, but she liked light colors.

She was a very bright, funny girl who didn't need much to laugh. Once she really started laughing, she could hardly be stopped.

She wore a silver chain with a heart medallion and a chain wrapped several times around her left wrist.

Most of the time she was barefoot. Her skin was already tanned from the sun.

Dan listened for a while and then said, "They are warning the other tribes that we are coming. That a little white magician is there and then they tell about the fire. That mine is stronger. And that I can conjure light that blinds them and burns their weapons."

"You're crazy," she said incredulously, but cautiously.

"Believe it or leave it. Me and the tribes they tell," Dan replied convincingly.

From that time the train was constantly under observation. Dan reinforced a few guards and they waited for the expected warriors.

Nothing happened on the first night, however, and it wasn't until the second night that a few scouts appeared in sight, without incident. On the third day they attempted to approach the camp, but when they had approached about 50 m the guards jumped up by a rope pull and innumerable puppets, made simply of twigs and clothing, or of hunted animals, rose to their feet.

Half of which were built to have an animal head but a human body made out of branches.

This time, too, the effect was not lacking, they let out a scream, dropped everything and ran away as if the most terrible ghost had asked them to follow him.

When they later arrived at the tribe's camp, a great commotion broke out, and everyone ran together to hear what had happened.

After the scouts' report, the council of elders was called together and they considered what to do.

But it wasn't long before they came out of the hut where the council was meeting and everyone was waiting for the verdict. The chief declared Dan taboo, and the penalty for disregard was the death penalty. In addition, it was decided to call the guardian spirits to ask for their protection and then the spirits should be asked what kind of spirit they had sent to earth.

Now they felt unsure whether they had attacked a good spirit and if it was rightly angry with them.

If necessary, a sacrifice would be made to appease him. It had also been established that death came only from the weapons of his companions. But he could have done it, since he also had such a weapon.

The questioning and asking began at the turn of the day, when the drums sounded again and people danced to ecstasy. The ghost questioner brought himself in full smoke, supporting the dance with rattles and drums, after a while he collapsed unconscious.

According to the tribe, he was now meeting with the spirits. The warriors now took turns dancing in a circle with the women around him.

The incantation ended at daybreak, and a stillness fell over the whole camp.

Now they had to recover from the hardships and all waited for the verdict about which ghost it would be.

Dan meanwhile left, with the obstacle that the blacksmith questioned all decisions, especially those of direction.

At lunchtime, both sides sat down.

The tribe awaited the verdict - the trek discussed whether to take another break or whether to ride through from now on in order to reach the destination the next day.

A tumult broke out among the warriors who were to hear the message first. Violent movements could be heard in the chief's hut, but no one came.

After an hour, the chief came out and announced that the spirits did not recognize the boy as one of them, but that he was being guided and protected by a great spirit of good. Also, the spirits said that he would become a great peace-bringing chief and that many zombies would come and destroy them all if they didn't make peace with him. However, he saw nothing friendly for his companions, he described them as destroyers, like spirits of dryness. He warned them not to meet unless guided by the boy.

Meanwhile, there was heated debate among the English.

"Who actually tells us if they are actually still alive in the fort, if they weren't attacked by a tribe and all are dead," asked the blacksmith and added. "We are too little to defend a fort."

"A pointless comment on the subject, how are we supposed to decide whether to go on without a break or move on without a break. They should have familiarized themselves with such facilities before we sailed from England. "Now it is important to determine whether we can all hold out, which I strongly assume from you. Up until this point they had wasted a mighty amount of energy trying to subvert since the change of leadership," the teacher replied.

"And now you're making a big deal out of your post, pah and now you think you have to teach us all something," the person concerned replied.

"Stop arguing, you're worse than children, so I praise my daughter. Dan must think he's taking some jealous kids with him," Nadiene's mother interrupted the argument. After which Nadiene giggled.

"I want a decision now, from everyone. If you don't want to drive through, don't get up, now and that goes for it," Dan said.

So it had to happen immediately and no one could wait and see what their pro or contra group would do. Even the blacksmith didn't know how to vote against Dan, since he didn't vote and also excluded himself.

Suddenly it wasn't an argument anymore, everyone wanted to come as soon as possible. Because apart from Dan and Nadiene, who now believed it, nobody knew what the drums meant.

After an hour they set off again, and the blacksmith again discussed how to carry it out.

The tribe now discussed whether they would have to appease the "man guided by the great good spirit", as he was now honorably called, or not.

"You can't give him a living gift because the others would kill him," said one of the council, without knowing how to answer the first question. But whoever spoke it had such an honor among the tribe that the first question was no longer pursued.

It was decided to ask a new warrior who had not yet had blood on him. And let him talk to the spirits. At first he resisted, not knowing whether he too should be a sacrifice to the spirits.

With the threats that he would die otherwise, he saw no chance for himself to escape.

"The one guided by the Great Good Spirit," said the warrior standing beneath the spirits, doesn't like victims, only friends."

One of the elders asked him, "What can we do that the others cannot harm us?"

"You can destroy them if they are not with the boy, but you must not harm the girl and the mother who have him in the wagon. But they are not used to the country either, and that can also insulate them." replied the warrior.

After saying that he broke down.

Slowly but surely the fort came into view and solid paths began, along which the poor crowd now moved.

Secretly the night spread over the country and a lion roared yawning in the silence >to say good night<.

Now you could already see a glimmer of light and large solid shadows in the distance. Gathering the last of their strength, they set out for the final sprint and the thoughts of how they would now be accepted had returned.

Dan was excited to see his parents again soon.

Dan's homecoming

When the trek arrived, it spread like wildfire. Everyone came together to see the newcomers and say hello to Tom and Dan. When they saw Tom's bareback horse with Dan and also his rifle, they grew quieter. The children knew that they couldn't speak to Dan today and the others also let the newcomers calm down.

At first they slept in the car. Only Dan went home and took his girlfriend and her mother with him.

The evening passed very quietly.

In the morning when the first roosters could no longer hold their beaks, the first tinkering started. They decided to eat together.

Now the sawing and hammering started again, just like the first time.

Travel experiences were exchanged while working, which could not be said during the meal.

Dan was with the mayor covering the trip. Everyone was dismayed at Tom's passing and sent their condolences to Dan and Fed. After that, Dan helped with Nadiene and her mother, and Fed also took some time to do it.

"I'm glad Dan was in the car with you. He should stay what he is for a while longer - a child - . He also found a friend in your daughter. His friendships are very loyal and strong. In England there was a huge farewell." Fed.

"I think that's good with Nadiene, it was no different. She's a little antithesis to Dan, not so curious anymore if I may say so myself. But a walking questionnaire that always wants to be filled out. I used to let her read a book once in a while. Since I worked in a library, this worked. Now I have to see how it goes." Mother.

"Were you ever married? I don't like to be indelicate, but…" Fed.

"Yes but my husband died in a duel with a Spaniard." Mother.

"Oh I'm sorry I'm Spanish but I hate duels. I'm here because of the stupid country duels." Fed.

"But here every day is a duel." Mother.

"More of a challenge and maybe it'll do something for Dan." Fed.

The conversation went on at work until the evening and the food was already being prepared.

During the meal there wasn't much talking anymore because everyone was tired from work.

Dan showed Nadiene the botanist's collection and, like a lesson, told some other things about each item.

When he didn't know anything else, she
looked at him with big, bright eyes. This time
the "big questionnaire" was also speechless.
The parents quieted down and smiled when
they saw the two.

A medicinal plant

The sun sent forth its first rays of light
without letting herself be seen, like scouts to
explore how they would be received.
Suddenly there was a knock on Nadiene's
door that woke her up and heard Dan's voice.
"Nadiene get up quickly you can have
breakfast with us before we leave." Dan
called without entering.
The door opened and Nadiene looked at him
sleepily from her little white nightgown.
"Oh Daaan you can't even see the sun
properly." Nadiene.
But he just said, "You look cute, half asleep
in your nightgown."
"I'm gonna come." Nadiene.
When she came she was totally changed.
Seeing Dan, her face was all smiles again,
she had tied her hair back into a small
ponytail with leather (fur-covered ribbon).
She was wearing a short gray blouse and thin
blue trousers for the planned tour.

"Come sit down, Nadiene, they'll be right there," Jenny said and put her bread and milk on the table.

Dan and Fed came and ate.

It was now morning and the three of them left hugging Jenny. At the gate, Ernesto, adventurer, was waiting for them.

He was Fed and Dan's biggest concern, but there was no stopping him from coming along. Fed checked his luggage and sorted out some nonsensical items, but others found his additional approval.

"You don't necessarily look like a rookie," Fed noted.

"Well I was on an expedition to find the source of the Nile once." replied Ernesto.

So, did you find it? asked Fed.

"No, we weren't very lucky. First yellow fever and then we realized that the natives' consent had not been obtained." The last came a little tauntingly.

They set off and soon all they could see was the steppe around them.

The children ran in front and they seemed to be recounting the last novel they had read. They talked non-stop.

"Hey little one, what do you actually orient yourself by, you just talk and walk as if you're getting something from the store for your mother," Ernesto called to the boy.

"I go by feeling." replied Dan.

"Great," Ernesto said sheepishly, hoping he wouldn't hear. But Dan smiled because he heard it.

Suddenly he put his hand on the floor, rested it for a few seconds and jumped up again, taking Nadiene with him, who was prepared for anything.

"Quick to the bush," he called.

Just arrived at the bush, Dan gently pressed Nadiene down when a great roar and tremor began, in the moving center of which a large flock of antelopes swept over the area as if they had been bitten.

Then the hunters came. Five lionesses chased after the herd.

"Oh no please don't." said Dan.

"What is it," whispered Ernesto, "they're not chasing us."

"Yes, but if they catch one, we'll have to stay hidden for quite a while to keep it that way." explained Dan.

"So they don't hunt us down," Fed said.

But they weren't lucky, but the lionesses caught 2 antelopes.

"Hehe, black day for the antelopes I guess," Ernesto said, but it didn't catch anyone, because they knew what it meant.

After a while Ernesto lost patience with the long wait, the lionesses had decided after their meal to lie down a little and watch the vultures devoting themselves to the rest of the meat.

"Why don't we just shoot them, there are only 5 and we are 3 with guns, before the remaining 2 checked us we reloaded again." Ernesto

"That would be human, yes, everything that stands in our way is just gone, but we think differently," Fed replied.

"But that takes so much time." Ernesto

"Why are we in a hurry?" Dan.

"No, but that doesn't have to be the case." Ernesto

"Nadiene, do you have a small hand mirror with you?" asked Dan.

"Now, no, I thought...." Because Dan realized that Nadiene now thought she had made a mistake or something, he put a finger over her mouth. He hugged and comforted her.

"Why do you want to scare him with there own reflection, to make them leave," said Ernesto, grinning.

"I have a compass whose cover is almost like a mirror on the inside. If you leave the lid intact..." added Ernesto.

"Sure, just trying to persuade the animals to find somewhere else to nap." Dan.

"To talk? You're joking, aren't you," he handed him the compass, ready to hold it up if he started running.

He took the compass and with the inside he kept blinding a lioness in the face.

At first she just kept trying to turn away with a grunt of discomfort.

She didn't succeed though as the shimmer always followed and played around her face. The goal was quickly reached, annoyed and completely unwilling, she got up.

As if on command, the others got up and calmly started to move.

"Well, I'd say you had the best arguments for her," Ernesto said.

"Yes, she didn't like my game, it's a pity I actually started to enjoy it." Dan.

"I can imagine that," Nadiene said, tickling his side and shooting out of the bush.

But she wasn't faster, Dan soon caught her, pretending to tickle her but didn't.

Hand in hand they walked back to where the others were already waiting.

After the luggage was picked up again, they went on as at the beginning.

Ernesto soon saw that this wasn't yet one of his beloved adventures, with a map and compass through undiscovered territory.

It looked more like a walk with incidents where everyone knew where to go but he didn't.

But he didn't get annoyed about it for long, since that wasn't all that new to him either, after all, at least the area was new to him.

Besides, they had told him that there wasn't a specific destination, so there wasn't much to look for on the map yet.

They walked like this for the rest of the day and the following. In time, Ernesto also began to tell stories.

He told what happened in England, that in America an organization called "National Geographic Society" was founded from which some expeditions went out. And above all he talked about his safaris.

Since it was already beginning to get dark again, it was decided to look for a suitable place for the camp.

Suddenly drums started beating again.

"Don't we have access and try anyway," asked Ernesto, dismayed, to Ferdinand.

"I don't know, Dan understands, I don't understand the signals yet." Fed.

"That's a win." Ernesto

"But I don't think there will be a problem as he's still running with Nadiene 10 meters ahead of us." Fed.

"For being a kid, we rely on him pretty heavily." Ernesto

"I should probably, he's the only one who still knows this area." Fed.

"Like, you don't know where we are anymore." Ernesto

-

"I'm not here that often," Fed said. "I usually don't go that far into this area, I prefer the western direction, but once you know the country, a couple of days safaris are no longer a big problem." Fed replied, grinning inwardly.

"You frighten me, since you all walk like it's just your garden, I haven't looked at the map where we are since a long time." Ernesto

"You can ask Dan, he'll show you where we are right away." Fed.

Dan and Nadiene stopped and waited for the two to catch up.

"We can camp here," Dan said.

"And the drums," Ernesto said nervously.

"Ah those, they're not so wild, they already know me and have been following us all day." Dan replied calmly.

It didn't seem to bother Ernesto that much anymore. He only casually asked what the drums mean.

"Somebody's sick, they're driving out evil spirits." Dan.

"Yes, I've already experienced that through this voodoo, a half-sick child jumped around alive and kicking the next day." Ernesto

"The Bible says faith can move mountains," said Fed.

"You really can't describe what they're doing as Biblical.", Ernesto replied, almost offended in his honor as a Catholic.

"No but the same spiritual law." Fed.

"Mmm hmmm," he didn't want to answer anymore, but made it clear that he didn't want to see it that way.

Looking for another topic, he noticed that none of the children were to be seen and excitedly shouted, "The children are gone."

"Don't worry, they're up there," Fed tried to calm him down.

"Where up there?" Ernesto

"There": Fed pointed at the treetop.

"That means Dan would like it to be a long night," added Fed.

"But they're still children..." said Ernesto, irritated.

"They just want to sleep for a long time, that's all, I think Nadiene will be very tired, she doesn't get up as often, as early as Dan. And besides - there isn't a safari where he doesn't. He really loves to climb trees and sleep in trees." Fed.

"Well, that's not so wild, as a little boy i sometimes climbed the tree while playing. So that means we don't leave that early tomorrow. That's good then I can write a bit in my route diary." Ernesto

When the children had finished building their camp, they came down from the tree and the food was prepared.

Nadiene went to bed straight after eating and Dan went a little alone under the tree.

"I'll check on my son, we don't normally do that, walking away from the fire alone." Fed explained, somewhat surprised and also somewhat concerned.

When he got to Dan, he saw that something was wrong. Dan cried.

Fed didn't say anything he sat next to him and just put his arm around his shoulder and held him tight.

After a while, Dan stopped crying. Knowing his son, he asked, "Are you thinking of Tom?"

"Yes." Dan.

"I think if he were here he would be proud of you managing this." Fed.
He laid his head on his father's chest and said nothing.
They sat like that for quite a while before Fed went back to the fire and Dan went to sleep. Ernesto didn't ask what it was, he figured it was something private.
"Since we left without a specific destination, we already have something specific in mind where we're going, looking for something or something, or planning a timeline, I mean, eh, I guess I don't know, they're not just doing it for their son's joy without planning a timeframe for such a thing." Ernesto
"No," Fed smiled, realizing that Ernesto was afraid he would really have to sacrifice importance at his expense." We go up a mountain to look for medicinal plants. A friend brought it for us and told us where to find it." Explained Fed.
"So we have to look for something, after all," his eyes began to light up completely again. It seemed as if this message had charged him with additional new energy.
"Well, but it's not necessarily like your search for the origin of the Nile, here we know roughly where the plants are." Fed.
"That's what the others meant too, with the comment - you just have to follow the river backwards. Most didn't even come back. Well I think - I hope it won't be that bad. - But it was unsuccessful after all that in the

end. People like me, you know, don't like it either. Of course we live for and with adventure. That gives us the "joie de vivre", and if some come back, where you want to be one of them, usually something new is always discovered, but the sponsors also want to know that their goal has been reached for whatever reason and - without sponsors there is no safari .

With your son as a safari member you would have a 70% better chance of finding sponsors just knowing he's been on a few trips and knows the languages..." Ernesto now blurted out in explanation.

"You have something specific on your mind?" asked Fed.

"Well, there's a haulage company planning to look for a forgotten city where the rolls of Phoenician shipping charts are hidden, on which is said to be a route by which they are said to have returned richly loaded, together with Israel." Ernesto

"Well I guess the sponsors aren't just interested in the cards to prove it, but also where the gold went or where they got it from. You figure out with the maps it's easier to find.

I figured something like that, but I don't think he'll want to. He doesn't like always having to test himself in front of adults because he's still a boy." Fed.

"I don't know, there are more people who have experience and therefore know when it's better to trust someone who is much younger. Actually there is no hierarchy apart from the "boss", the members are usually selected according to what they can do and that becomes their task and when something is discussed, everyone's opinion is taken into account. I've seldom heard that when a woman was there, she did night watch or something. Dan is almost a complete expedition in itself." Ernesto

"You can ask him tomorrow." Fed.

Suddenly it seemed as if a skeleton was approaching from afar. Ernesto was about to jump up, rifle in hand.

"Easy, he just wants to see your fear, they enjoy seeing you scared so they're not scared. Then again, he didn't want to make it that strong or you wouldn't have seen him before he got close enough to throw a lance. I'll get Dan I probably only understand half of it if he talks fast." Fed.

"And what do I do in the meantime, you really don't want to leave me alone with this." Asked Ernesto almost in panic, not really reassured.

"Make a gesture for him to sit down, invite him for a sip of water." Fed.

Fed disappeared, meanwhile Ernesto trying not to shake too much.

The warrior arrived before Fed returned with Dan and Ernesto stood up, forgetting everything Fed said to him. So they were just standing in front of each other when Fed arrived with Dan.

Dan smiled knowing how Ernesto must be feeling. Then he went to the warrior, exchanged a homemade antelope figurine for a copper bracelet containing many hunting symbols as a welcome gift. It should bring good luck to both of them when hunting. Then both settled on the exchange, knowing the other's enduring goodwill. The warrior didn't get that close to the fire, wanting to keep the effect of scaring the others.

After drinking some water with Dan, he hastily began to explain the reason for his coming.

Fed waved Ernesto an acknowledgment that he had already lost the thread of this conversation.

After a while both only realized that Dan was resentful about something and the warrior seemed to be begging him with everything. Then came Nadiene who noticed Dan's absence.

Everything seemed to change, the warrior tried to apologize several times, but everyone who heard anything about Dan knew about a probable existence of a girlfriend of Dan. The fact that he had nothing for her seemed to make everything else worthless and he could probably lose face.

Dan didn't really take it that hard, not that he didn't want Nadiene to have something, but he didn't see it as a need either. But in order not to present her as worthless, he took part in the apology hearing.

Fed soon noticed and motioned to Ernesto not to make any violent movements and to remain seated.

Nadiene, who understood a little what the two were talking about, quickly understood the situation and became very insecure, she didn't know what to do. She hid in the background with Dan's father.

But that only fueled things, the warrior now thought, either he had scared her, or he shouldn't see her for a reason that was his fault.

As Dan realized things only got harder the longer it went on.

He had once seen a judgment made and a branch broken over it to confirm it as a seal. Of course he didn't know if it would work here, but he tried.

Finding no branch within reach, he did so; "Since you didn't bring anything for Nadiene, I ask, because you want us to come with you to help you. That you, you give something when we're with you and the next time I need a great warrior, you work for me." Dan.

Then he pulled out some blades of grass and tore them in two. Unintentionally he cut himself, which the warrior did not see at first. But the ceremony impressed him so much that he no longer dared to question anything. Then he saw the blood on Dan's hand. For him, Dan was placed high, like a shaman, the

fact that he was bleeding now made the fear
quickly return to him. It was like Dan had to
bleed for him, but the deal was made. Since
blood was the symbol of life, he assumed the
spirits would decide his life belonged to Dan,
so he did whatever Dan could to make it as
comfortable as possible.

Dan got up and explained the situation to the
others, and they left.

The dream of sleeping in the tree house with
Nadiene was over.

When they arrived in the village, silence fell
very quickly, the drums faded away as if the
drummers had given their utmost and their
strength was slowly fading until the last one
seemed to have no strength either.

A woman wanted to quickly move Dan into a
hut, but the elders refused her.

She was very nervous. The village medicine
man hissed at Dan from the side, to him it
was like he'd failed the spirits and now he'd
been taken to do his job. Dan tried not to
flinch, but Nadiene jumped, which displeased
the warriors but seemed to give the medicine
man ample satisfaction as he backed away.

Then the elders, Dan and Nadiene, entered
the hut with his father. At first the elders
wouldn't let Nadiene in, but Dan wouldn't let
her go.

In the hut lay a boy whose leg was badly
swollen, the air was very difficult to breathe
as it was full of the scents meant to drive out
evil spirits.

Since no external wounds could be found, Nadiene said that her friend once had a fracture that hadn't healed well and something was stuck and that it had to be broken again in order to heal properly.

Fed felt the leg and indeed found poor bone connection, which did not appear to have fully healed.

After several discussions it turned out that the boy had worked too fast again.

"It can be explosive, the fracture is still too soft, but it should be broken again. Then if that's broken wrong, it might get worse," told Fed.

"I think your medicine man knows enough about that, let's say he has to break it back in the same place and put it back together properly. And that the leg is then free and wants to heal, only that you have to be careful that the evil spirit of impatience doesn't enter the mother. Nadiene, how long did it take with your girlfriend?" Dan.

"I don't know, I haven't seen her in eight weeks." Nadiene.

"Well then, let's just say that he has to stay in bed for 8 weeks." Dan.

"Not a bad diplomat," said Fed.

Then they told the elders to go out with the mother and for the medicine man to come with a strong man.

The mother refused strongly, but they drove her out anyway. The medicine man proudly entered with another strong young warrior, knowing his skills would be in demand.

When Dan explained what to do, he sobered his pride very much. He noted that ability was required, but also what failure could mean.

The price of his service rose very high in his mind.

Dan and Nadiene left the shack, begging the medicine man and the others to stay, unsuccessful, not even wanting to hear the boy's bones breaking and his pain.

When the work was done, the warrior came out of the hut, covered in sweat. But to the displeasure of the others, he couldn't say what's going to happen to the boy.

Then Fed and the medicine man came out of the hut too, they had tied the boy's legs together and then wrapped him up tightly to the waist on the bed.

The medicine man was very angry with the mother and demanded a quarter of all the results of a year's work.

This hit the mother hard and the warrior who seemed to be the boy's father was also devastated, but nobody said anything.

Since Dan did not ask for a price, it was decided to give him a bracelet made of worked gold and his father to wear some gold pins that others wore in their ears. But they gave Nadiene a necklace made of ivory splinters, which also contained some gold parts.

Calm returned, but the village, which had been agitated by drums and dances, now seemed deserted. Only in the distance could the usual sounds of the African night be heard. The next day, too, it took some time before life returned to the village.

But children are unstoppable. So it was the children who romped around first, until the adults woke up from the noises of the children.

Then the work began. The women fetched water with a few girls, everyone knew their job, so there was not a single discussion or counter-question from the children.

A hunt was prepared for the men, and Dan and Fed were also invited to the hunt, which they accepted.

Someone had seen antelopes and they wanted to hunt some and if possible be back in the evening, which was not always that sure.

Usually it was two or three days before the hunters returned to the village.

But this time they wanted to have a party in the evening to honor the guests.

Nadiene also wanted to help with the preparations, but they politely declined, as she was a guest.

Hunting was something else, it was seen as an honor to be part of a hunt, it wasn't just chasing an animal and then having meat on the table. It was a contest of strength and endurance against that of the animal. Will an animal lose its life to continue to guarantee the life of the villagers?

The hunter had the right to eat the first choice of meat from the animal he had killed.

When the first women came back with the girls, the hunters took water and set off.

It was a short hunt, the antelopes hadn't gone very far from where they were seen, after a few hours of following the tracks they were found.

One snuck up against the wind at spear throwing distance, so that the spears had an "equal chance" against the guns.

Suddenly an antelope started looking up and seemed to notice the hunters. This was like an unspoken signal to the hunters to shoot, whoever wasn't close enough had no luck in this hunt chasing a fleeing animal on foot usually took days.

But the hunt was successful, not everyone was lucky, but everyone seemed very satisfied with the success.

Each hunter took his dead animal on his shoulder and they went back towards the village. Dan's antelope was carried by another hunter who was unsuccessful that day. The hunters were good runners and didn't seem to mind the onset of the midday heat. Fed and Dan, who were getting used to walking in the arid, hot steppe, were beginning to have trouble following.

Suddenly one of the hunters began to sing a song, which was repeated psalmically by the others.

It was a song in honor of the antelope, it spoke of an antelope proudly escaping a hunt by the leopard.

The strength and beauty, as well as the speed of the antelope, was extensively described in many words.

The singing made it much easier for the two to run and it seemed as if the strength and speed of the antelope would come into the legs of the runners. The hunter's legs also seemed to fly now, as if they didn't have time to touch the ground.

A song was then sung in honor of Dan, Fed and the medicine man how they cast the evil spirits out of the boy's leg last night and now the boy's leg can heal.

Later other songs were sung, about the steppe, about the sun that goes to sleep at night and gives new strength and warmth the next day.

In the meantime the village could already be seen from afar and after half an hour's walk they would arrive.

It pleased both of them, who began to feel the tiredness of their legs again near the village, the songs had made them completely forget to walk. Dan was already disappointed that they would then fall silent in the village. But he was also happy to see Nadiene again.

The village seemed deserted from afar, everyone was hiding from the heat.

When the hunters were spotted by someone from the village, everyone gathered to receive them. A surprise had been prepared for Dan.

When the hunters arrived, the women and girls began barking, as was the custom, to show their joy.

But this time Nadiene was also with the girls and women. This showed a full effect of surprise on him. He stopped when he spotted Nadiene among them, spoke her name and then ran straight towards her, hugging her and spinning.

Now the barking broke out again over the two accompanied by the laughter and giggling of the young girls.

For the Africans, these gestures were enough to signal togetherness.

And so it was not surprising that later some women asked to organize a party for the two. It asked some interpretations to explain to them that they wanted to wait a little longer.

In the meantime, the antelopes were fully prepared. Even the meat that was for days later was processed immediately. The hard-working women and girls walked over the animals like a swarm of ants, leaving nothing unprocessed.

After that, everyone hid in the shades of the huts again, fleeing the late-midday heat.

In the evening a drumming began to announce the festivity. A fire was lit and in the large square in the center of the village, the village seemed to have doubled in number of inhabitants.

The drumming got stronger and the first ones danced to the rhythm of the music.

Anyone who hadn't slept a little before by now was too late and a long night of drums and singing began.

No one was spared from the rhythm of the music, even some old people seemed to be getting their youth back.

Nadiene and Dan also danced along, so Ernesto said he had never seen blacks allow white children to join their dances. But with them it was different they had healed a boy from their village and hunted and sang with them. To them they were now, some of them, like family members who lived a few days' journey away. And it promised to stay that way unless one attacked the other.

The festival lasted almost half the night and the next day it was not surprising that the first ones did not emerge from the huts until early noon.

A day later the four continued their journey and two days later they found the medicinal plants they had set out for. Others were also taken that were of good value.

On the way back they visited the village again, stayed another night and told a few stories, some of which lost any chance of being credible. But they were loved to listen to because the moral of the story was good and they were very interest and joy taking in. The next morning they left again to say goodbye, the fact that children were already singing songs about Dan and Nadiene let everyone know that they should probably never be forgotten in the songs.

So it was not an easy farewell.

On the way there was silence until Nadiene asked something. Like a spring reaching pressure to break through the last slab of granite, the children's usual seemingly unstoppable conversation erupted.

"It's like paradise so alive and free when you see and hear the two children like this, an image that I think everyone would wish they had, had in their childhood. I know I'm still chasing much of what I'm hoping to experience most of what the world has left for me, but free dissolution seems so unattainable," said Ernesto, taking this as a sought-after opportunity in a conversation to begin as if the children had loosened the chains of silence to him too. It seemed that Ernesto found more than he thought in this expedition, which looked very different and less promising. Yes he had found the real reason. The reason that drove him to all these adventures.

Not that it was wrong, but looking it from a different perspective, it could also make you feel sorry. Was his problem, the problems of many human, having lost sight of beauty and carefreeness through cares and responsibilities.

"Yes, I know what you mean, and I'm actually happy every time I'm there and can participate. It's like a part of me can be young again. It is the art of being able to switch off from all your worries and to be in your dreams. What Christians describe as an opportunity to 'become like children' and to trust the God they trust as their Father to handle all difficulties for them. You may see the problems, but don't worry about them. It's like a child coming to its father in pain, trusting that everything will be better afterwards. So they have enough time and thoughts for joyful things." Fed.

"And you can do that? - I mean, what if we screw it up between him and our mistakes and stuff, or out here.

You don't pay attention and the lion is there. He just says bon appétit." Ernesto

"Well most parents don't say no to forgiveness to a child they love and you may have seen at the beginning Nadiene and Dan were yards ahead of us talking non-stop and yet it was Dan who gave us the warning the pack of antelopes hunted by lions." Fed.

"And if you don't listen to the signals, that's good appetite and one to zero for a lion." Ernesto

"I've also heard how enemy soldiers marched past each other and only realized what was going on when they were at the same height and nobody fired. I think that anyone who can have the freedom of trust of a child can only do so if they are as fortunate as those children are." Fed.

The next few days passed without any problems, they talked and walked home. Sometimes the children would start singing and the men would often join in as the Africans did on their way from the hunt.

So they got into the fort, which had meanwhile grown into a city.

There was already a great commotion there, as they were expected to return long before that. Nobody knew about the incident in the native village. So they were then overwhelmed with many questions.

There have been versions of the blacks or the wild animals being killed, but this was laughed at when telling the story of the lionesses that Dan blinded.

Then someone said, "I guess she didn't like the direction you showed them with the compass", which caused a lot of laughter from many.

Dan then took Nadiene into the house, who didn't seem to have a chance to stop laughing for a while. When she stopped, her stomach did hurt a lot. She had to start all over again when she saw Dan and thought about the lionesses.

But since Dan also knew this, he made every effort to prepare the herbs for the apothecary.

Burning air

For a long time nothing happened, you went about your usual activities and the children struggled in the heat, at school.
It wasn't that unusual, but nobody wanted to take it for granted.
It hadn't rained in months and the water capacity dropped to almost zero.
Even the lions often came close to the city to look for easy prey among the domestic animals.
One morning Dan and Nadiene came back home.
"Today we don't have a school, the school is closed, the teacher thinks it's too difficult and some people can't make it anymore." Dan.
The mothers looked worried because the children had been given extra water at school, which they didn't have at home.
"OK you can play then." Jenny.
But she mostly said that so that the children wouldn't notice the concern she had.
"What do we do now, because of the water in the school, they had water at least three times a day," Jenny said.
"Yes, I don't know either, Nadiene had already felt dizzy twice, she didn't say anything, but I saw it.
Dan was very scared yesterday. We just need rain, I mean the natives have been here for

centuries and they don't live without water either." Nadiene's mother.

"I haven't seen in all those years that we ran out of water."

The next day just got warmer and so it lasted for another three days.

Suddenly the alarm bell went off. It was fire, a wooden house had simply caught fire in the heat and started to burn.

Some quickly began trying to put out the fire with water and it took some time and conviction to stop them.

"We can't take water to extinguish, try to save most, but without water we have nothing to drink.

Think of your children." Mayor.

It was hard but true, it's not easy to suddenly lose everything. Standing there and not being able to do anything. But it was true that a lot of water would be needed and the chance of saving a wooden house in the dry heat was simply too small. It was decided to meet in the school building in the evening to discuss what can be done.

So most of them arrived at the schoolhouse early in the evening.

The teacher was entrusted with the leadership and that's how he started.

"Without much fuss, as everyone knows, what happened today can happen again any day. We cannot extinguish fires because we cannot use water to extinguish. We need it for ourselves and the animals. We also have many sick people due to the lack of hygiene and since yesterday we have already had 3 deaths. What can we do?"

"Yeah, I don't know either, I used to take a lizard and give it salt. They always found water. Last time she rolled over and died." Dan.

A murmur of horror and helplessness broke out.

There was a lot of discussion and consultation, and at the end the blacksmith said, "I can't give any extra water, but I have a house made of clay and stone. I can give a place to someone who has a wooden house, so if his house should burn in an undesirable way, everything is safe for him."

This was taken with great praise and approval, and without persuasion, the others followed his example. It was organized who would stay where. The school was also made of stone and was planned as accommodation. In the end, however, they still found place for to isolate the sick.

The next day the parades were underway quickly, everyone was happy about the great solidarity that someone said it was just a pity that such a common working day could not end with the usual good common bottle. An old woman gently hit him on the head with a pillow, "no water but think about drinking." she said approvingly.

Everyone tried to cheer up and forget the worries of the rainlessness. No one succeeded, everyone felt it too strongly in there own body.

The nights began to get terrifying, it was pleasantly cool and almost ironically cold, but the hyenas weren't far away after the first casualties. And her laughing and barking didn't really let anyone get any rest.

That night even a lion looking for one last easy victim in the city had lost to a few hyenas.

"Strange the beasts always make it," said one of the guards.

"Well, they drink too," replied his companion.

"Man, that's the idea, where can we drink that too."

"Are you sure you want to drink blood?"

"Uh no".

The next morning the children got up and came down the stairs.

Suddenly there was a rumble, Nadiene had fallen down the stairs and remained lying powerless at the bottom of the stairs.

Startled, Dan stood motionless without saying a word, like a lifelike doll.

The two women came running and Fed, who was standing outside the door, rushed in because of the outcry to want to follow Nadiene's mother.

He immediately put Nadiene on some skins and took Dan down the stairs to prevent him from collapsing from standing for so long and put him on the bench. As soon as his father let go of him, his whole body started shaking.

"Jenny wrap him in a blanket and hold him, he's in shock," said Fed, "I'll see the doctor." With that he walked out the door.

Nadiene's mother held her in her arms, crying and nervous to keep asking her to come back - wake up again.

When the doctor entered with Fed they were accompanied by the bell alarm, again costing a house. But the owners were happy to have put everything in a safe house. So they only watched over that the fire stayed at one house.

In the house, the doctor first checked on Dan and switched to Nadiene when he realized that Dan had fallen asleep from exhaustion. He just looked Nadiene in the eyes and felt her pulse.

"I can't do much, she's not sick, but she doesn't have any strength because of the lack of water. I'm sorry."

Then he took a closer look at Dan, also feeling his pulse and looking at his eyes. He didn't say anything, but you could tell from his expression that Dan's condition saddened him as well. The two mothers held their children as if to protect them from someone who wanted to take them away from them. After a moment of silence, the doctor asked Fed, "I know Dan learned not to need as much water on the steppe, but how long has he been without drinking?"

The three jumped in shock. "They both always got something to drink in the morning and around noon."
"He has the symptoms of not drinking for at least a day. Not just as if it was the last time yesterday at noon." Doctor.
"But I always gave them both something to drink," Jenny replied again.
"Has Nadiene ever fallen over or maybe she just got dizzy?" Doctor.
"Yes, twice," her mother replied
"Did Dan see it?" asked the doctor.
Nadiene's mother just nodded, head down, feeling guilty about Dan's poor condition as well.
"Then we just have to make sure that he drinks it too," Fed replied, wanting to end the uncomfortable subject.
"But on the other hand, he carried through Nadiene's life," assured the doctor.
That day it was very quiet in the house and in the city until evening they counted 5 dead, two children and two old people, one died because he gave everything to his children and drank nothing.
In the church, the pastor had already called for the third evening of prayer for rain.
Fed also went to prayer every evening with the two women and children. This time they had wrapped the children in a blanket and placed them on the bench during the meeting. The meeting was simple, praying a few psalms and encouraging one another in

praising the Lord with past prayer testimonies.

Then a man came forward with half a cup of water and said, "See, I saved it for you, because when my house was burning down you protected my belongings, my wife and children, that you gave me my friend's house for protection .

Thank you for that," said a other. Then he put the mug down on the table.

It was decided to give the water to a three-year-old girl who was in danger of not surviving the night. The evening was continued for three hours with prayer and Bible verse reading. Anyone who had a verse that somehow gave courage did read it loud. What was accompanied with thanks to this situation and help. Many stayed in the church that night

At sunrise there was a knock on the church door, although the door was not closed.

At the entrance there were a few natives who didn't dare to enter, they snuck into the town where the guards had fallen asleep. Now they didn't dare to go in, they were afraid of the great spirit of Dan.

When Dan saw them he wanted to go to them and got up, but collapsed after a few steps.

The thanks and the memory of the healing of his leg, the black boy, were stronger than the fear.

The boy rushed in and gave him water from what they had brought with them. The warrior had now pulled up all his courage and entered. Then they wet the children's faces and slowly fed them until they had drunk almost a liter. Then they left the rest of the water there. Keeping only a part that they felt they needed for themselves. The boy broke an amulet into three pieces, tied one piece around Dan and Nadiene, and left the third one on himself. Before the guards were relieved and it was noticed that they were asleep, the natives were gone again, as if the ground swallowed them up.

Everyone was speechless for a while. Then they thanked God for this help. The remaining water left by the natives was distributed to the other children in the town who were near death. There was no death that day and in the evening the church was full.

This happened twice more on different days. The third time the boy said they couldn't come either because there was nothing left to share. By then no one from the town had died, but everyone was in the church, even the guards kept watch from the church tower to attend the gathering. After three days, when the first children became dangerously weaker again, there was suddenly a noise as if a water hose ripped open over everything and the water suddenly splashed down. It was raining as if the clouds were in a competition to see who could drop the most water to the ground, as the fastest.

A great rejoicing broke out, the children were taken outside and some began to dance outside.

They behaved like children who were allowed to celebrate Christmas and Easter together and so they celebrated for 3 days.

The joy of surviving the drought was simply indescribably great for everyone.

The natives also celebrated days, which usually began in the evening and ended in the morning.

They sang songs and danced the hole night.

The land had its joy and life back, even the sounds of the animals were fresher and livelier.

All the sounds of lamentation and torment were exchanged for those of joy.

Then the restoration and rebuilding of the destroyed houses began. There was constant music at work due to some natives working in the town. They sang songs about rain, ancient myths and about a great house that the Great Spirit will build on the earth in which all peoples will dwell. They were beautiful songs, full of joy and strength, without complaint. The lead singer didn't put a hand to the work, which everyone agreed with since he needed all his strength to sing out loud. But with every syllable he sang, he seemed to be challenging the followers with more strength.

Anyone who understood the native language soon knew the history of the tribe and its myths.

It was like a history lesson in which the students simply had to sing the text after it, or the singing reminded them of the good old days.

So it didn't bother anyone other than the teacher, who used the technology for his history teaching. They just thought it was funny because he wasn't used to it and didn't have a particularly loud voice. With the second song, the lead singer took pity on the teacher and repeated everything in a strong voice before the others repeated it in chorus. Sometimes you would hear laughter or a discussion about how naïve one or the other king or general could be.

One of the carpenters then commented that he never thought of teaching English history and his hand partner replied, "Tell me something, I never thought I'd be taught anything by a teacher."

Now the days of working together were completed again with eating together. Some stayed together longer and told each other about the good old days or made plans.

Others just sat and listened, enjoying the communal atmosphere.

When the work was done, a delegation of thanks was formed to visit the native village, taking useful gifts such as jars and pots.

Everyday life returned and everyone went about their work.

Part 2

The search for the Phoenician travel parchments

The arrangements

By now Dan was 15 years old and because he spent a lot of time with his native friends, it wasn't so unusual that Nadiene and Dan were now also married and had a son. They were now living together permanently, with Fed and Jenny. Nadiene's mother also lived there now, so she wasn't left alone.
The fact of having family responsibilities didn't seem to have destroyed a spark of vitality in Dan and Nadiene.
On the contrary, working hand in hand made the parents appear a little younger again.
The people in town were already saying that Christian, or simply called Chris, would become just like his parents.
In fact, he began very early to examine everything from his cradle.
A caught greyhound quickly fell victim when Chris, no one knew how he got his hands on

it, was found disassembled into a few individual parts after his examination.

Both began to teach how to survive in the African outside world, know plants and animals.

One day Ernesto sat down in the background with the students and listened, but actually just waiting for the end.

But after a while he also began to ask questions with interest, so that at the first question the children turned in surprise and looked at him like a wonder of the world. He got a feeling of insecurity, but the questions were all serious. Dan and Nadiene just went to him, shook hands and hugged the old friend. The questions were answered and interpreted seriously in front of the class.

At the end of the class, they greeted each other properly.

"So you are now giving classes on survival techniques, you look good, and now you've grown quite a bit." Ernesto

"You look good too and it's good to see you again, welcome back to Africa," Dan greeted him.

"Oh nonsense, look good, I'm afraid I'm getting old." Ernesto

"Ah, you still have time for that," Nadiene replied.

"And how do you look, the travel routes of the ancient Phoenicians already found?" Dan asked him

"Well, that's actually why I came. Let's talk about this in peace. Here's a chance to get something nice to drink, school always got me so parched." Ernesto
We start a fire and relax and laughed together.
"Why don't you just come to our place for the day, we'll just drop by the store. You know we don't have alcohol." Dan.
Nadiene looked at Dan questioningly and he added, "I think there's someone waiting for you to meet you."
"Meet me, who?" Ernesto
Both just grinned, but didn't answer.
He was also warmly welcomed in the shop, as he was still well known.
"I'll come and get a bottle from the crates I brought you."
But when he paid and was about to leave, the manager tapped his arm, put a glass on the table, filled it and said, "On the house."
Then they exhorted him not to forget the evening to visit them. Which he accepted.
"It's fun to see old friends again, to know each other and to see good memories.
It makes you feel at home there, too."
Ernesto
"Yes, I felt the same when I was back at the port where I picked up my first trek with Tom. We sat in there for a long time, talking new and old, like Tom did for the first time."
Dan confirmed.

"Surely with the one difference that you were dead tired the next day." added Nadiene with a smile.

"That's right, the next day was a horror." Dan.

When they entered the house, Fed was standing in the middle of the room, turned around, and said, "Aaah, well, if that's not a surprise. - Jenny we need one more plate, you won't believe who's there."

She came out of the kitchen to see who was coming to see them.

"A what a surprise, how are you?" Jenny.

In the meantime Nadiene's mother had also come.

"Thank you very much and I hope you too."

"Yes, thanks."

Then suddenly a baby murmur could be heard behind Ernesto.

He turned around in surprise. Nadiene held Chris in the arms hugged by Dan. Both beamed happily.

"Well, who do we have here?" Ernesto asked the question, looking at the little one, but of course asking Dan and Nadiene. They answered as if in chorus, "Christian, or Chris for short."

"Well, Christian, will you be my new colleague?" Ernesto

He only got a murmur as an answer, but he bent too far over him for that and the asked one then held on to his vest with all conviction. There were buttons that he didn't know yet and it was a firm plan to examine them.

He elicited a laugh from everyone and Ernesto said, "well, you can count that as a sure yes too."

"What else can you expect, they say like father, like son, and if the mother is like that, then what other chances does the child have," laughed Fed.

"Yes, you may be right," Ernesto replied with a smile, freeing his jacket again in the meantime.

The women went back into the kitchen, with Nadiene putting Chris back in a place covered with skins and fenced with wooden lattice.

"Sit down," Fed said, pointing to the bench at the table.

"Thanks, I hope you don't mind," Ernesto asked, placing the recently purchased bottle on the table.

"Go ahead," said Fed, calling to the kitchen to ask for a glass.

But it was unnecessary, Nadiene came with three glasses and water and put it on the table.

The three thanked her before Nadiene disappeared back into the kitchen.

"Boah, it's hard to believe how grown up the little talking waterfall has become," said Ernesto looking at Nadiene.

"Ah, that hasn't changed, the two of them still talk non-stop when they're alone, no idea what the two talk about, but they always have something." Fed.

"Things like news and all," Dan replied.

"But you guys are together all day. The few moments when you're not there can't be that much conversation." Fed.

Dan just grinned.

"How is old Europe doing and how are your travels doing?" Fed.

Dan was no longer interested in Europe, he had been living in Africa for 9 years now and the only thoughts he had about Europe were picking up the newcomers from the port and then giving courses so that they had the useful knowledge they needed to get along in Africa. For him, Africa was his full home and he didn't care about politics.

Fed, on the other hand, remained interested in what was happening in his old homeland. Then he started talking about the expedition.

"Well actually, to be honest, that's why I'm here. A group called "London Research" has now formed, made up of sponsors and scientists for this cause. Lectures on the Phoenicians are given at the University of London. Well, as a member, I've been telling them about our last tour together.

Most people were interested and now I want to ask on behalf of the committee if we can recruit you to take part in this expedition. Of course it will be paid for."

"It sounds interesting, but who do you mean by you?" asked Fed.

"Actually, I was thinking of you both and Nadiene, but now with the baby, Nadiene was probably not going to happen.
We don't know how long it will take."
Ernesto
Nadiene, who overheard it, was now disappointed, he was right, she can no longer simply go on safaris or expeditions.
Now they had a child, probably the courses will be the only thing for a long time, combined with the memories that she had left of this lifestyle.
Everyone felt sympathy, everyone knew how much she would have liked to come, even if it didn't start until the baby was weaned. It was the hard point in life that you can't have everything. Now Dan also realized that she had actually not been out of town for a year. It made him unsure whether he too should stay with Nadiene, or should he go with them and leave them at home, no matter how many researchers the family had.
He knew that researchers often died on an expedition. He knew the way from the port. Not the route of the expedition. Neither do the tribes they may encounter. If he goes now, maybe they'll come back another time, there were many expeditions in Africa. All these thoughts went through his head and for the first time it was not easy for him to decide.
Then Nadiene sat down on his lap and said, "You are a trek leader a born explorer, I

knew from the start that you don't stay indoors. You should go - for both of us." She said it softly and gently to him.

She knew that he would give it up for him, but she also knew that he would then change, that he just needed such tours, a kind of elixir of life. She knew it would happen one day, only that it was now – made her sad.

Ernesto now felt a little uncomfortable in his own skin, he would have preferred that the decision didn't have to be made yet or that it was already made. He played nervously with his glass.

Then Dan asked, "roughly how long is the expedition supposed to be, I mean if you assume these roles are in a certain place, you can plan a time."

"We expect three months." Ernesto

"So five months," Dan thought out loud.

Ernesto thought he didn't get it right and wanted to correct it.

Fed signaled that he understood and knew what he was saying.

"When is it supposed to start?" Dan.

"If you are clear." Ernesto

"We have to wait another three months." Dan.

"The hottest season of the year," Fed joined the conversation.

"Well that's really one reason, I think we forgot that summers get a little hotter here than in England. It was just thought that by the time we set sail in England at the end of the summer, we'd be a little bit used to the heat." Ernesto

"How warm was the summer in England?" Dan didn't remember it that way.

"Oh forget it, it was probably the dumbest idea." Ernesto

"No, I don't think so, but it would be interesting to anticipate," admitted Fed.

"We had 83 degrees Fahrenheit now we have 10 more at the moment. How was the boat trip, it got warmer for you too.?" Dan.

"Well it worked for me, as you know it's not my first trip to Africa, besides I'm southern Spain." Ernesto

The last one came with such pride that everyone laughed.

"Well, to decide, I want to see the group first, not that it's the first time guiding people through Africa who didn't know anything about Africa before. But I know the area where you want to go I only know the first 10 days". Dan.

"Do you know everything within 10 days?" Ernesto

"You also know your front yard and back garden, aren't you," said Nadiene.

Ernesto almost burst out laughing, "the joke was good, if I had such a front yard or back garden in Málaga or both, I would be so rich that I probably wouldn't be here."

Dan looked at him inquiringly and said, "naaah I don't think so, you'd probably be one of the sponsors going on your own sponsored expedition."

Ernesto looked at him in amazement, then grinned in reply, "and I think I'm caught." Then they laughed again, making Ernesto and Dan blush.

They still told the news from the city and what you heard and knew from the village and so it was a day that went late into the night.

Ernesto stayed with them overnight and when he woke up the house was almost empty of people.

Jenny was the only one still working in the house apart from Chris when he went downstairs.

"It's so quiet here, has everyone flown out?" Ernesto

"Well it's already 10 o'clock in the day. Did you have a good sleep?" Jenny.

"At this point, I almost don't need to say yes anymore. But thank you, it was just perfect." Ernesto

She put some bread and cheese on the table with water.

"Thank you. When will Fed and Dan be back?" Ernesto

"They usually come for lunch around lunchtime, but Dan and Nadiene said they're just going to get Chris and go eat. I think after the info yesterday they want some alone time." Jenny.

"Does that mean he's coming?" Ernesto

"Well he said he wants to look at the group first but I think he's counting on it. We had a drought here once, even with deaths. Nadiene was almost too.... Well after that, since they were kids, they'd been together every minute. They love each other so much that they are together every moment they can. Not that they never argue, the first time we thought we'd never see Nadiene again. But when it got quiet, we didn't see either of them. They then sat arm in arm, we were told, by the river for hours. Then in the evening we heard her come in the usual way, talking like a waterfall. After the second or third time, Dan would often jokingly say "Miss Wautenso" to Nadiene. Wautenso is our family name. You have to say they got married really early and we didn't want to agree at first, but then again, everyone was expecting it." Jenny. Around noon everyone came back to the house and greeted Ernesto and asked how he was doing. Which he always answered with, Well, thank you.

Nadiene and Dan wrapped Chris in a blanket, laid him in a cloth, which Nadiene then tied around the front. Acting like a tote bag in which Chris looked out and could move his arms.

Then they said goodbye and left the house. Ernesto didn't want to ask anything about the expedition, but talked to Fed about the planning.

In the evening Fed then urged Ernesto to stay with them until the expedition would start. He didn't agree easily
and it wasn't settled until Fed and Jenny accepted a small fee. Ernesto didn't want to insult the hospitality he was offered, but he didn't want to accept that while he got money for such expenses, which the others also spent, Fed and Jenny shouldn't give anything. Nadiene and Dan came back very late, only Fed was awake, which he always was when someone was out.

"Dan I think it's a little bit late after we stayed up late yesterday and you'll have to get up early tomorrow as well. Also, it's a little rude to just leave Ernesto without any information about when you want to watch the group. I think it would be right if you apologized to him tomorrow Dan." Fed

"Yes sir, I'm sorry." Dan.

"Come on tell me. Did you guys have a good time?" Fed.

"Yes thanks," both replied.

"Well, that's good. Let's go to bed now, tomorrow is another day." Fed.

The next day Ernesto also got up early, not wanting to miss Dan this time.

He came to him with Nadiene and apologized for yesterday.

"Oh no, we're friends, aren't we? That's the romantic thing about love," he replied with a slight grin on his face.

"We have a small information reading in the afternoon, for the last newcomers your group is also cordially invited. - In the evening we have an offer for a table for free in the restaurant, if everyone eats there too.
Then you can lay out your project for us and we can then discuss it in peace." Dan.
"That sounds good to me. Will let the others know." Ernesto
His father nodded in confirmation and also proud that he hadn't forgotten.
"We've also been invited to Square Spring for the weekend. I said maybe you'll come too, so the others can get a little taste of Africa for those who don't know it yet." Dan.
"Great, what's Square Spring?" Ernesto
"Oh sorry, forgot you didn't know. Three hours from here a couple of natives have settled down to work with us. But they want to keep their own way of life." Dan.
"So, big party this weekend." Ernesto
"Yes, do you remember the boy whose leg we saved? He now wants to marry his second wife.
We'll have to talk more later, duty calls." Dan said pointing to the clock.
"OK, so see you in the afternoon."
In the afternoon, the schoolhouse was packed with people, full of expectations of getting everything they needed for their new life.
Most of the languages were Spanish-Portuguese, English and French, but there

were also a few in Polish, German, Swedish and other languages.

The teacher who ran the school wanted to send the children out first. But Dan let them stay, followed by the remark that he probably wanted to teach a second Dan.

"That shouldn't be necessary after Christian," replied Ernesto, who came in through the door and heard it.

There was a lot of questioning and discussion that in the end it was agreed to take three other evenings after the weekend.

Towards evening they gathered in the inn. Nadiene was also invited and Jenny at the group's expense. So Chris was also present in a basket in the corner with Nadiene.

At the beginning, before a professor presented and explained the theories and plans, they thanked them for the afternoon, which was also instructive for them and almost everyone was present.

Dan and Fed quickly realized that some things had to be translated for a Frenchman.

"Thanks for the interpretation," Fed began, "First of all, I think we all have to agree, monseigneur vous besoiron aprondre anglaise, if it has to be translated to watch out for a lion or duck your head in front of a snake hanging from a tree , I'm afraid, sir, you might be dead one day."

Most found the remark a little harsh, as there was some mumbling. But everyone saw it immediately.

"Furthermore, I would have liked to see how resilient everyone is. I don't want us to say that if it doesn't seem absolutely necessary, for example, we still have to climb the mountain today, that it's no longer possible. In the end one of them collapses and we have to wait days. Any leadership decision regarding the march will be made by my son Daniel and accepted by everyone. If he says no more today, then we hold. If he says we'll take the pass, then we'll go, or he says until then today, then we'll do it even if our backpacks are already dragging on the ground.

He will also be the best at warning you, of animals or the like, that there is still time to hide or whatever he says to do. We go looking for the roles and not hunting or anything like that. He also chooses the people to help us carry your gear. If you decide from a scientific point of view you need a sample here and there and you have to stick to him."
Fed.

Then he thanked them for listening and gave it to Dan.

Dan grinned and started to chime in, "I hope no one comes along later and says they wet their pants because after all this they didn't dare to say they had to go." He smiled at that. "But no joke, I should know if we have to stop for that too, that's a better way to know that one has the honor or dishonor to serve as a souvenir for some tribe. - Who can sing everything, no great arts, just sing." Dan.

Fed and Ernesto started laughing. They already knew what he was up to. But the other question was very surprised.

But some got in touch.

"Well then we're not so little. Who has ever been to Africa - steppe and, or jungle?" Dan.

Few responded to this question, so Fed and Dan were a bit shocked.

"This can be difficult," Nadiene said to Dan. Everyone realized that this fact didn't speak very well for them. Finally Dan said they will have an educational next 3 months.

Then they discussed the organization of provisions and equipment.

After the meeting, Dan told Ernesto when they got home that they probably have one problem person in the group.

"Well, I think the Frenchman will have learned enough English in three months, I think." Ernesto

"I'm not thinking about, I'm thinking more about, it seems to me, the investor, Simon. Never been to Africa, no experience of any expedition, but makes enough claims." Dan.

"Yes, that's highly likely, but unfortunately we need his money. He's a 40% investor, but we've already said it's far from being a vacation. Back to the main question, would you guide us?" Ernesto

"How is my family secured if something happens to me?" Dan.

"Dan!!!", Nadiene got a little scared at the question.

He took her in his arms and whispered, "I don't plan on staying out there somewhere, but I'm not resilient... ."

Ernesto felt it wasn't the right time to answer this question and just nodded to Dan.

They went to sleep and the next day Dan and Fed got a good offer for their families which they accepted and at the same time put them in charge of the expedition.

Then came the weekend at Square Spring. Entering the village, the scientists who accepted the invitation noticed the popularity and fame of Dan and Nadiene, as well as their parents. Ernesto was recognized immediately and greeted warmly, even before they were really there and had greeted everyone, one of the children grinned and started a song about the four of them, which was sung with Ernesto on their last visit as a farewell.

It sparked right away with Ernesto and without further words he joined in.

"Now he's really back," Fed said to Dan, who nodded in agreement.

Some women and men expressed their respect, to Dan for Nadiene and Chris.

It was a credit and honor to Dan as head of the family. But they also did it deliberately in front of Fed, as a token of appreciation for his upbringing and family leadership.

They also greeted the scientists and exchanged gifts. Ernesto literally soaked up the atmosphere, and that's how it happened that at the end of a song he kept singing a new one from the ones he still knew. It didn't take long before he found himself as lead singer. Of course he didn't remember the lyrics one hundred percent, but it wasn't a problem, a boy quickly found himself on his knee and helped him sing.

Suddenly the teacher, who was one of the townsfolk who had come along, started laughing out loud. One of the villagers wanted to know why, maybe to be happy with him.

"Oh, I just remembered, looking at Ernesto, how we rebuilt the houses after the drought." Teacher.

He remembered well and knew he meant his audition, which was reinforced by one of them.

He quickly sought out the lead singer who found it an honor to resume these alliances. When he then came to the teacher, he still felt a little unsure, so they talked him into something else until he agreed.

As the teacher began, it was now clear to everyone that there was no need to bother with the musical entertainment.

In the evening, drums joined the singing. The evening trembled with singing, drumming and dancing.

Chris also seemed to pick up the rhythm when Nadiene gave him her milk. He followed the rhythm with his legs and Nadiene had to take him away from her chest a few times to slow down his over enthusiasm.

This time Ernesto was also invited to take part in the men's dance.

"Gladly, but I assure you that I will be the biggest embarrassment in this dance." Ernesto

He then grinned and threw himself enthusiastically into the ring of dancing men, watching Dans dance closely, and after a while he too got into the rhythm of the dance. Encouraged, two other young scientists also wanted to join the dance.

"Wait," Jenny said, "you can only dance if you're one of them, the dances give other opportunities for the man"

"But Ernesto is one of us, and dances too," replied Jack.

An Englishman and adventurer like Ernesto who would not miss anything that is unknown if he only knew when and where it takes place to taste it or to participate.

"Ernesto has been invited, and he has held the tribal honor since his last visit." Jenny.

"He must have made a powerful impression back then." Jack

"Well, they saved the life of the young man who is getting married tomorrow. I think also because he also remembered the songs and

you got the introduction as lead singer."
Jenny.
"I can 'imagine me self now why Ernesto was
so bizarre after the last trip," said François.
"I can imagine now..." corrected Jack.
A warrior said he should take a woman who
speaks English, then he doesn't need to learn
it, she will translate everything for him. They
laughed both. Then François said that he was
married and had four children, one of whom
died of a fever two years ago in the winter.
The warrior then asked why, since winter is
the best season.
It was difficult to explain to him that it was
colder there and even snowed.
"Come to me with your family in the winter,
I will build you a hut and in the summer you
can go back." Krieger
The explanation that it was summer in France
when it was winter in Africa failed, but he
seemed to understand that it wasn't that
simple. However, he insisted on maintaining
the invitation anyway.
Now he invited him to the dance to show this
joy to the spirits.
"There's no such thing," Jack said, "he can't
even speak proper English and now he's
being invited to the dance."
Nadiene and Jenny laughed. "Yeah, what a
pity that you speak English," said Nadiene,
laughing out loud.
He felt a little uncomfortable at this
comment, but then saw how François was

struggling to keep up and decided that maybe it was his salvation too.

As it got late, some scientists began to wonder when the wedding would start tomorrow, that if it lasted and started early, nobody would get much sleep.

"You probably won't sleep much this weekend," said Nadiene, "but you can still sleep tomorrow at noon, in the midday heat there is total peace here. It's too tiring in the heat. You will also notice this on the expedition."

And that's how it was, in the morning there was only a light meal and finishing with the preparations that had not been done until then. Around noon, with a heat of 40 degrees, everyone stayed in the shade of the huts, where most of them slept again.

As the heat began to subside, the last of the guests arrived.

Suddenly the bride started singing with her friends. There was a rapture of the bridegroom's strength and skill, and much adoration of his looks.

The children started making jokes about it, sometimes using the children's names. of a boy which often has looked up to a girl or something like that. Then an elderly woman called for silence among the children.

Then came the bridegroom, accompanied by his friends, among whom was Dan. To pick up the bride from her parents and her friends.

Against a promise from the bridegroom and confirmation from the bride, the father then left his daughter in the hands of the young man, then the spirits were asked for their favour and he took his new wife into his hut. The women began to yell loudly, Nadiene's mother startled when she saw Nadiene with these women.

Although she had heard that Nadiene could doe it but was not thinking of anything about it.

After a while, the rhythmic dances began again. Dan had taken precautions with François this time and definitely taught him a few typical moves. The celebration broke every limit of time and it was not until late in the morning that things quieted down. So Dan met Nadiene, who was already asleep, holding Chris lightly on her chest. He woke her up holding Chris to prevent a startle reaction.

Nadiene got a little shock too. Afraid that Dan might be angry, she tried to apologize to him several times. After all, other African women were left alone because of such things and the child was taken away.

Dan put a finger over her mouth and tried to calm her down. It was already too late. She started crying, she was just too tired. He hugged them both and when Chris was done they went to sleep.

They only came out of the room that was set up for them a day later.

Then came three hard, warm months and two of the scientists gave up, they had fallen ill and only wanted to go back to Europe once they had recovered.

Thomas the "Investor" showed more strength in the heat, than anyone expected, which put Dan at ease.

The Departure

The long-awaited morning for the scientists had dawned, the day before the natives had arrived to help carry the luggage.

Dan and Nadiene had been awake for a long time and were sitting on the small staircase in front of the house. They talked at first, but when Fed stepped out of the house, he found them very still, there arm around the other's waist, just enjoying being together.

Fed realized that the days of non-stop talking should be over. They had now discovered the quiet, gentle togetherness, a togetherness of understanding without words.

Suddenly, in Fed's eyes, the image of the little but actually almost restless son disappeared. Suddenly he noticed how time had passed, a journey he was allowed to experience without noticing the time. But it gave him everything back at once, like a wake-up call in a beautiful dream.

He had to sit down for a moment.

When he re-entered the house without disturbing the two of them, Jenny was a little startled. The fresh yet young look from the smile watching the two talk incessantly was gone from Fed's face.

Jenny had felt it before and realized that Fed now saw it too.

"Yes, he is an adult now. - You are still awake, but now you can also enjoy the power and romance of silence. Your father said the same thing back then. He also said, 'Ferdinand has now discovered a new world that doesn't need any strength, but gives strength if you don't stay in it too long and forget your goals. It's a relief because now I can see a bright future for my grandson."

Jenny.

Then the door opened, Nadiene and Dan came in, accompanied by François.

"Good morning, I hope I'm not disturbing you, we talked a little and your son invited me to breakfast with his pretty nice wife. Of course only if..."

"Sure do us the honors please," Fed and Jenny replied almost simultaneously, grinning at each other at the fact of unity.

They sat down at the long table while Nadiene and Jenny brought food and water.

"If I think like that, it's almost impossible to mistake me for a Frenchman. I'm just starting to speak English and from today I won't be drinking wine with dinner for a while."

Francoise

They laughed it seemed to mean something if French people don't have wine to drink.

"We'll reserve one for you return," Jenny promised him.

When they had eaten, they prepared to leave and went out where some of the men were already waiting.

After everyone had arrived, the last check of the luggage and the big farewell came, which was not without tears for some. The men left town ready, ready to discover and conquer the unknown.

Joy flowed through the veins and changed completely with the thoughts of the farewell that they had just a few minutes ago. Now the thirst for adventure was awakening again in the men, which seemed to give them the strength to find whatever they were looking for, even if they had to traverse the entire globe to find it. Everyone wondered what kind of valuable treasure they were going to find.

No one could and would not hide their mood, everyone started joking about legends of hidden treasures.

No encouragement was needed that day, it was amazing what they put through on the first day.

Nobody seemed to notice the heat.

After a few days the euphoria subsided and Fed and Dan tried to make the men forget the heat and exertion with the African singing choir. It didn't work for everyone. François had a little trouble following the lyrics to sing them, but he didn't bother too much. When someone told him that he was behind with singing, he just smiled and said. "I form the echo.- Have you ever heard an echo heard at the same time as the original."

Jack laughed so loud that even the others looked, then he said, "let's sing the echo together."

Jack was mainly in helping François by teaching him English, now they had become good friends.

Then Fed said that François would have to teach them a song in French too. But they decided to start with a simple one, which then became "Master Jakob". It was then translated and sung in English, German and Spanish. It later became the expedition's wake-up song.

First days in Africa's jungle

Individual trees began to be seen from afar and the air began to get fresher. It was a welcome change, most had lost interest in the songs and every step seemed to stretch into a mile. Now the strength began to return again, everyone wanted to reach the fresh variety as quickly as possible.

When the first trees were reached, Dan had the whole group stop and lie down under the shade of the trees. Everyone wondered if they were now motivated again to go on. But Dan didn't answer the questions, he sat down a little to the side, took his compass and seemed to start playing with the inner mirror. Ernesto sat down next to him, but left him without a word for a long time.

Then he asked, "what do you think, we can't use everything and have it, bloodless like by the lions?"

He didn't answer, only his face showed that this was exactly his question.

Ernesto leaned back and gazed dreamily into the distance.

Suddenly Dan stood up and said, "We just have to find something else," stabbed under an approaching scorpion and threw him far away. Indignant, he resumed his orientation and went on his way.

Dan motioned to his father and to Ridschard the leader of the expedition, asking them to come to him, meanwhile unrolling the map on the ground, on which he sat down again. The two asked met with Dan and Ridschard and asked, "what's up."

"Well according to the map we are here, it took us a little longer than planned. The last few days seemed to have asked for a little more strength than we expected. But we also have to look for other things now to get out of confrontational situations without hurting anyone. So far I've bet on the sun, which is good for blinding opponents. But this will now be covered by many trees. By the way,

the climate asks to take the medication by your people.
Well there are two possibilities, there is a village marked on the map about a day's journey from here. We can say we leave here early in the morning and reach the village in the evening, so we can say that the first night we are still within sheltered walls. Or we'll go on now and then we'll have our first night off in the jungle, we only know about the residents, nil anyway." Dan.

"Well that's an interesting question, I don't think this should be decided by us alone." said Ridschard.

"But we still have to think through all the options earlier, then we can make more precise suggestions, I think. Right? - I mean, we can also get acquainted with the local people if we walk around during the day. Maybe they are enough not to be afraid of us, or aren't." Dan.

"With the last one, it shouldn't matter whether we continue hiking or not. What tells us that they don't visit us here, too," admitted Fed.

"Do you think we should keep walking and try the night there?" asked Ridschard.

"We have to do it anyway, we can't always count on ending up in a village that wants us or is still there. Some villages have simply been abandoned on their way to becoming cities," Fed replied.

"They could also have built on a elephant trail and for some reason the new one didn't appeal to them and they go the old one, then the village collapsed. I just wanted to explore a few possibilities, we're in an area that neither of us has been to in the past week. But we have probabilities that might be worth considering. I mean who tells us that tomorrow we'll make it to the village. We don't know any obstacles here, they are usually not always marked." Dan.

"I think Dan, if you explain it to the others like you did to us, then they will have a sufficient overview and be able to decide. - On both sides you can also ask if you want to know something else. Then we can still provide information when we know," said Ridschard.

"Well then, let's get them together," Fed said, nodding to Dan.

They encouraged him this time to just sit and wait for the other two to get the rest together. He let the others see that Dan was in charge. Fed would have liked to see it all from afar, just proud to see his son leading an expedition. But he was in the middle of the expedition. Now he thought he had the feeling Tom must have had when he saw little Dan leading a whole trek. His thoughts wandered, he could now imagine what kind of first impression Nadiene must have had. He was slightly disappointed, he would have liked to have watched that too. Suddenly a voice snapped him back to reality. It was François, he just asked him to come.

"Yes, sure I was..." Fed.

"Don't say it, if you say it, it's as if it's over and you don't think about it anymore, maybe you can keep your feelings a little longer that way." Francoise.

François was a good recognizer of character, sometimes he just looked you in the eye and it seemed as if he could read everyone's mind, even feel their feelings. They went to the others without saying a word.

Actually nobody really wanted to know the possibilities. They had already imagined that they could count on everything and were therefore interested in completely different points such as water etc. When they thought that there was enough water, they simply decided to "take the rest of the day off".

The next morning, as was customary, the "wake-up song" - "Master Jakob" - was heard. It was sung in Spanish first, as the last guard, Alberto, was a Spaniard. Everyone who woke up answered the question, are you still asleep, his no and then started singing along.

After a small breakfast, the small group began to drill into the jungle until it was finally completely swallowed up by the same.

It was a big change, not only did you feel fresher as the heat was still there.

So it seemed to be more alive, they were totally new sounds. All of the jungle's wildlife seemed to continue to announce their arrival. Not that there weren't any noises in the steppe, they were just quieter and rarer. It surprised some how Dan could still hear the individual animals and occasionally show some.

Sometimes it was amusing how the animals behaved before they disappeared.

One came with bananas handed Dan and Ernesto who were walking together a few and Ernesto said.

"Man, this is paradise here, you only need to pick up the things and eat them."

"Yes and you also have some plants here that heal a lot and more. Or you take a banana stick and oops, something bites you, well it was a tarantula. Maybe you still have a few hours to eat your laps before it's over."

Ernesto said, laughing but serious.

Disappointed, the other left the two alone and Dan could only call out, "Thanks for the bananas".

"One of us died from something like that back then, we just didn't look. Well, no one knew, everyone was new to this area and to Africa. The leader who knew Africa died of fever before we were in the jungle. Now our naivety to go further had cost many lives. There are many cities on the Nile, we said to ourselves, that should work." Ernesto

"But it hasn't deterred you from coming to Africa again and again." Dan.

"No, but I asked around more last time who it is who I'm going with. Admittedly, at first I thought it was your father guiding us and thought it was because of you two. No real adventure tour should be right from the start. Well, this time, I came to you." Ernesto

Yes you are I don't know there are now some who run safaris or take people to new cities, some I hate, they run safaris just to kill animals. They don't even eat the meat, just for the fur or the head or whatever. They're really destroying my country. --- I don't know, I can remember when we came here. We wanted, or rather my parents, just tried to start somewhere else, just a chance to build something up. Today - they're coming and the land is already theirs anyway and the natives should be glad THEY are coming. Not all are like that, but too many are. What is it, after all, everyone is human." Dan

"You know, all cultures had that, for example there were many oriental empires that had come to Europe. A high culture becomes so rich that everyone can afford more space. But it's not there, so it's taken somewhere else, where you're not that far. Well, they then think that state law should be bought with progress." Ernesto

"Daniel in front are a few statues with their heads upside down in front of their feet or are missing altogether, at least the porters don't want to go any further," reported one from the expedition group.

"What does my father say?" Dan.

"He sent me to you to come take a look at this."

"Ok". Dan.

Dan looked at the statues, "he should have gone to the doctor earlier, his teeth are a little long and he's got horns. I think the statues have been neglected."

He went to the natives and spoke in Swahili, speaking quickly but in a calm tone. He didn't want others to understand him, but wanted to have a calming influence on the wearer.

They were very nervous and arguing so it took a while for Dan to get them to move on.

"We've lost a lot of time now, haven't we?" asked him Ridschard.

"It still falls within, I always count on a few small deposits that you don't know beforehand. It gets interesting when this pass over the river does not exist on the map. According to the map, there will be a river in about 2 hours' march. Perhaps more of a stream is drawn than a meter deep. But it appears to be about 100 meters deeper than we are now. If the bridge has been as neglected as the statues, then we need to be back up on the other side at least today, otherwise there's a good chance we'll have fewer porters in the morning." Dan.

"So it's already dangerous if we go further?" Francoise

"I don't think so, but they're scared enough of the old statues that maybe some would run away tonight if they didn't feel so safe." Dan.

"I'd like to know who put those statues up there, it doesn't look like primitive, at least to a certain extent." Ernesto

"Now who knows how far the Egyptians or the Israelites under Solomon went in Africa and left their temples or the like. Nor can it be said that people with the same level of culture did not live here. Only the condition of the statues makes me strongly believe that the constructors of the statues no longer value the meaning." Dan.

The jungle got denser and they only made slow progress so that they didn't reach the creek until around noon, but Dan's fears were correct.

All that was left of the bridge were single planks tied to ropes on the other side, hanging down to the ground.

What to think of this? asked Ridschard, Fed and Dan.

"Well, unless we want to go straight back, it's that way, downhill. - Be careful when descending." Fed answered with a grin.

"I'll talk to the porters, you'll be amazed how quickly we can get to the other side. But I would want each of us to wear something," Dan said

"OK, I'll pass this on to the others and make sure the burdens are evenly distributed," Fed replied and started walking straight away.

Dan went to the natives, "Well like I said. It's all deserted here, but once we're on the other side, those who put up the statues can't reach us. The others will also carry something, so we're a little faster, but please make sure nobody falls or anything, it's not too steep." Dan.

"Will we take a break on the other side?" asked Naru, his friend. "You're always behind, but up here the last few meters were quite exhausting and when we're back up on the other side - I mean..." Dan.

"I'll see if we can stay the night there." Added Dan.

Then the descent began, Fed had decided differently to carry the burden. They were lowered on ropes and the men only had to carry their weapons.

During the descent, some young Africans developed a desire to compete over who was first to the creek.

Dan got carried away by this lust too.

So the men raced down the slope, half-flying, barely touching the ground. It was a moment when they could let go and switch off. But courage also returned to them.

"Your son isn't a bad runner, it's good for us to see that city life doesn't exactly encourage such stamina." it was Jack who almost ran too but then decided the times were over.

"Yes, but he won't win, there are two in front of him, Tom, who taught him all this, also trained him very well before he went out of the fort with him for the first time. They are actually both very athletic, Nadiene and Dan. I don't really know such situations from the two of them, when the goal, or a goal was in sight, the running started, at first we were almost shocked. The two didn't have to agree on something like that. That's how it was then. If they had little or no luggage, they would suddenly start running.

You have to imagine that, the animals that could be heard from afar suddenly start running and that when you already had your goal in mind.

So we had no idea if something was coming or what was going to happen..." Fed.

"What did you doe?" Jack

"We ran after them like the hunted. When we arrived, out of breath, they looked at us innocently and wondered why we ran like that. I would say Nadiene's totally innocent, questioning face saved the two of them from possible discussions. If it had been like that, when on the way back the city was already in sight or something like that, we might have thought it by now. But it was just a point that we had previously identified on the map to rest there. There was also a big tree, which was enough for the race." Fed.

"Yes, I can well imagine that now, I think after a few minutes looking at the children indignantly, maybe I'd like to have them 'eaten' alive, I would then think I'd laugh at how different carelessness can be at that age ." Jack

"Well, we made provisions. Next time we told them to leave their luggage. We said that way we know and they can run better. Now we don't care if they run with or without a pack, it's safe to say that when Dan runs without saying anything to warn you, he's just running for sport." Fed.

By now they too had reached the bottom and the youth were having a good time. François was also in the sprint. He hadn't occupied a great spot, but he didn't seem to care. He was so fascinated to have had such fun again.

Now no one could help hearing how his legs seemed to fly over the little bumps and how light he felt. But they also rejoiced with him. In the meantime, everyone had become so close and well-known that they were happy about the fun their partner had or simply shared.

The creek was really not deep, they took the loads on there shoulders and crossed it with little effort, which the stream current demanded.

They had almost all reached the other side when suddenly the water started to move. From afar you could only see a black shadow and small bubbles as if the water was starting to boil.

It was getting closer very quickly and those who saw this apparition cried out in fear, shouted, "Get out of the water".
But the last one, an archaeologist, hadn't made it. Crying out in pain, he sank into the water, the stream turned red and after a few minutes it was completely still again. Only the man's skeleton reappeared. The shadow was gone in the same quick fashion.
Everyone was horrified, shocked, some had even bathed in the creek.
"Those were little fishes," Dan whispered, totally distraught.
"Piranhas - they eat everything," answers Ernesto
Fed and Dan hadn't expected anything like this, they didn't know this kind of fish. It made the two very silent as they climbed back out of the gorge.

Strange townsfolk

Nobody asked for a break anymore, the stream had refreshed them all, but also the death of the archaeologist left nobody in the mood to stay there for a while.
After a good while proper paths were visible again and it gave everyone hope that the town was near or at least not deserted.
Then they came in the evening. One could see the shadows and outlines of some buildings in the middle of a mountainous rise.

"Well we can walk through and would probably get there late at night, or camp here and run in there tomorrow," said Dan, seeing that some of the people were already very tired.

"No one sees their goal before their eyes and then suddenly stops," Ridschard replied.

Fed nodded approvingly.

"But there are no lights of fire to be seen."

"Maybe we just don't see them yet," Fed said. But Ridschard took the decision out of there hands. By showing the city to the others and mentioning that this was the city that Dan mentioned yesterday, he created in the others the idea that this was today's destination.

Dan felt exhilarated, which increased when sight of any fire failed to appear when they were about a mile from town. It made him feel like something was wrong.

When they entered, the city seemed totally deserted, not a living being to be seen.

They decided to investigate what had happened on the next day and camped in a shack on the outskirts of town.

After a little silence, a roar and screeching broke out, which startled everyone and covered their ears at first.

Then men suddenly appeared who seemed to make the only difference between apes that they carried swords.

"Great, we just needed something like that," said Ridschard

"This must be the species Darwin was looking for as a bridge between man and ape," said one anthropologist.

"I think they've fallen behind a bit in their ability to communicate," added Fed.

"Anyway, they're blocking the exit and we don't know how many there are," said François.

"Why don't we pretend we don't care until tomorrow anyway. They don't seem to think we're unarmed or they might have gotten inside by now. So 2 should be enough to keep an eye on the door. If someone shoots, everyone is awake anyway and we can be sure that our porters will all be there tomorrow." Dan said and lay down again.

"He's got nerves," Jack stated, horrified.

"But he's right," Fed agreed.

This reaction was not expected from the others. They stood there dismayed, but not daring to enter.

After a while they started with monkey-like screams, which woke up those who had already fallen asleep.

Suddenly Dan took the gun, shot it in the air and yelled, "Shut up, nobody can sleep, you have to express the room fee more clearly, nobody can understand that!"

He stood chalk white, dust and bits of ceiling falling over him. He fired directly over himself.

Startled and dismayed, the men backed away with their swords.

Jack had to start laughing at what he was saying, the fact that none of the others would have understood, and the mishap of firing the gun directly overhead.

This reaction seemed to provoke anger in the others, they came back screaming, but when they saw that a lot of these things were suddenly pointed at them, which bangs and can break stones, they stopped in a flash.

"Well, who's to say, let's go to sleep." Dan. Dan couldn't be stopped from showing no fear and just going to sleep.

And indeed they could sleep, only soft sounds could be heard at each changing of the guard.

The next morning they were gone again. Reassured, they got up and ate something. But when they came out of the house, they were horrified, these people knew fire.

Around the whole city was a ring of fire.

"It's illogical. There's no stopping you from going out of town, rather coming into town," Jack said.

"Well, I hope one possible reason why you might not be right isn't," Ernesto replied.

'What do you mean?' Jack

"Everyone gets hungry at times," Fed interacted.

"Bad end to an expedition," said François.

"No wonder they can't talk when they eat everyone up," admitted Ridschard, who only got half of it.

"Anyway, I'm not that interested in my point of waiting for another night and finding out who's right," Dan interrupted the conversation.

"Maybe we can fight the fire," suggested Ernesto.

"No, it's gas or oil that comes out of the ditch." replied Jack.

"stone ditch --that's good," Dan said, and trotted off.

"Well the boy is good but not very talkative," stated Ernesto.

They followed him, who took a closer look at the ditch.

"It's gas but I think gas from oil. There might be a lot of oil down there, but what's burning here is just the gas.

If we cover a large wide part we should have a narrow passage, fire will only burn as far horizontally as long as the gas pressure to the side is strong enough, which depends on the outflow pressure," suggested Dan.

"Which, in turn, is compounded by the pull that increases gravity, which doesn't necessarily cause the gas to rise directly." agreed François with a grin.

"OK Lecture over, let's start," Ridschard broke off the conversation, obviously annoyed, and went off to give the others instructions.

"Wow he's obviously not in a good mood today," Jack stated.

"Normally if we had followed my suggestion yesterday there would be an 80% chance that this wouldn't have happened," Dan said.

"Why?" the three asked almost in unison.

"I had my premonition yesterday, which signaled me not to go into town at night."

"Why wouldn't you, did you see something but didn't say it?" Jack asked him.

"You won't see him not raising concerns," Ernesto defended.

"No, I didn't see that of what we have too much now." Dan.

"Fire, but it's a good thing the city wasn't on fire." replied Ernesto.

"Fire gives light and people have normal light in the evening." Jack interrupted him.

"Yes, that's logical, why didn't I think of that too." Ernesto

"Never mind, you're good." Jack

"Hey," he punched him lightly on the shoulder and ran.

After a while they had completed enough to leave town.

The Temple

Then it seemed to be a really carefree expedition. Nothing happened for three weeks and it almost seemed like a hike. If one hadn't forgotten to take his fever medication, he became sick and infect some who were taking their medication but were struggling easily.

In the fourth week the man died.

"Africans asked me if you don't trust Dan, first about the city and then his death. Everyone knew Dan really wanted you guys to take quinine," Fed told the scientists.

"But it's not that, every one of us knows he needs that stupid stuff, had I known he stopped I would have stuffed that into him personally." answered Ridschard.

"Well, and I told you about the city, that was my fault too, but the fact of the matter is that they don't want to work anymore without knowing Dan's decisions."

"Well, that's anything but cheap, he's sitting up there on the hill and considering to give everything to you Fed. He thinks he's not a good enough leader and he's now responsible for two deaths. Nadiene would have been right. Don't know what he meant by that." Ernesto added.

"Oh, that's serious," Fed said sadly.

"May I know more, too?" Ridschard asked angrily.

He didn't like the whole situation, according to their plan they wanted to be on their way back for a week or two, now they're not even there.

Fed looked at him and said calmly, "She said exactly what the natives accuse us of saying it's deadly. Now we have dead people and there could have been more in the city."

"I think we made a promise..." Francoise

"Forgot," Jack corrected him gently. "Yeah forget, we all give him a big responsibility. He's good at it, but he's still very young, when something goes wrong even a leader needs the support of his group to build him up.

It was the people closest to Dan who went out to talk him down.

While they were talking to him on the hill, Dan suddenly said sheepishly, "Tomorrow we're going to the temple."

"What temple?" "What temple?" 'Where?' The questions got so jumbled and overwhelmed that Dan just showed through François' legs. who immediately looked around.

The men's eyes began to shine like a child who has been given a large teddy bear.

In the distance two stone pillars could be seen with a gray background amidst the bushes and trees.

"It must be the temple. I mean it should be around here, it just has to be this one." Ridschard almost over joyed.

"tomorrow Ridschard, tomorrow. We'll find out," reassured Jack, even excited.

Everyone had been waiting for this moment ever since they started dealing with it in England. They just enjoyed the sight for a while until Dan decided to go within 50 meters of the entrance today.

"Really you sure?" asked Ridschard excitedly Dan looked at him uncertainly, said nothing.

"I mean well, it's great, wonderful, let's break the news to everyone else." Ridschard.

The others grinned but said nothing.

"What is something wrong?" Ridschard.

"No why' Jack asked.

"You're grinning at me like that without words." Ridschard.

Now the laughter really started, everyone knew what they were thinking, but they just grinned at his delight.

"OK," Dan said, walking down the hill.

"OK, that's all, man we're exploding, almost exploding with joy and he - I mean, uh... ", Ridschard was dismayed.

"Why were we laughing, first we have to be there and get their roles in our hands, then I'm sure you'll see all the joy that Dan has. Am I right," asked Ernesto, Fed.

"Well I think the greatest joy remains sharing everything with Nadiene, conversing with her, over and over again." Fed.

"Yes definitely, on the black target, I think we should set aside a day for that too when we get back," François suggested.

Everyone else fully agreed with this.

When they arrived at the bottom, the others gave them a coffee. They looked at each other questioningly, they thought to start marching right away.

Fed held Nahum a porter, "Coffee?"

"Dan says we'll drink coffee and eat in an hour we'll leave, go to the temple," replied the addressed.

"He wants to run through," Fed stated quizzically.

"Yes, that's when people stay calm the most. They know they are almost there, which will give them enough strength.

Also, they now know that they need to rest properly and gather strength. And for people like us, that we don't have to nervously ask when we're going to leave. Which would be repeated during a break," Ernesto replied.

"It's clever, I've seen a lot of leaders almost lose their cool at the breaks because of something like that." Ernesto.

After an hour they left. The mood of the first departure returned, the strength, joy and pride to be there. The conversations what a treasure that could be.

The bearers shared the joy in their own way and began to sing.

Towards the early evening they arrived at the planned distance and Fed had all the equipment checked.

Dan looked at the function of the devices with interest, his adventurous curiosity, which was interested in everything, rose again to the fullest. He didn't rest until he, too, fully knew the functions.

"Fed, if your son keeps asking like that, all we had to do was let him come here alone for work. We would only have come along out of adventure and a love of research," François called out to him.

"Why aren't you," Dan called back.

There was a loud laugh and Jack said, "Fed how did you do that when he was little?"
"Well, we're having a lot of fun at home. When we moved into the house in the city, we came back from the first town meeting in the evening and found him in the middle of the hall, asleep among all the things he had brought together from all corners of the house up to that point."
"Yeah, I'm glad Chris won't have that chance," Dan admitted. "Cleaning up the next day was less interesting."
"Did you remember where you got everything from?" Jack asked, suppressing his laughter to a grin.
"That's why I don't want to give Chris the chance, no, but for me it wasn't that much of a problem, we chose the places we wanted." Dan.
"I haven't looked at it that way, I'd say lucky." said Fed.
"Oops." Dan.
There was still a lot of laughing and talking late into the night. The fact that they had reached the temple relieved and delighted them all. They talked about their childhood or funny stories from their universities where they gave readings.
Toward morning they set out to go to the temple in search of the notorious scrolls. James a cartographer set about making a sketch drawing of each corridor and room.

The aisle got narrower and lower, it was impossible to walk the aisle side by side or upright.

Suddenly, a huge flame shot towards them, but didn't reach them.

"What now we can't even see the end of the corridor and there's no other way but through the fire which no one can," sounded François disappointed.

"Let me see something," Jack forced his way through. "Something's wrong with the fire, it's not getting warmer. With the intensity of the fire, it must be oven hot here." Jack

He crawled on and didn't seem to get burned by the flames.

"Very effective," Ridschard admitted.

Suddenly Jack cried out from somewhere behind the fire.

François and Dan crawled as fast as they could to see what had happened to Jack.

Suddenly they fell about 2 meters deep in a small room.

"Don't get up," Jack yelled, pulling Dan down. A metal spear shot over them and smashed into the other side of the stone wall with great force.

"Boo, madness." Dan was shocked.

They called out the situation to the others and prepared to hold the others under the spearhead.

Ridschard looked at the system with interest. "Interesting technique, first it tests if you believe everything you see and then the best way to survive is not knowing what's coming."

"What do you mean?" asked Fed.

"If you figured out that the fire is just an illusion, you keep walking because of the light, you don't see anything and you fall in here. If you rappel, you don't have enough speed to get past the lances in case you don't know about them. You should look around before you get up though to keep yourself alive," Dan explained.

"He's right we should use all our senses," Jack replied.

They crawled into the next aisle.

"There must be more to it than just traveling rods on parchment," said Simon, "otherwise it wouldn't be worth all the effort."

"Usually temples have gold and such, I wonder what the scrolls are supposed to be doing here," Dan replied.

"They probably wouldn't be here either if the Phoenicians had stayed with the Israelites. But according to history they didn't, and legend has it they were laid here for both of them," answered Jack.

Which then suddenly sagged again, but according to his noises he enjoyed a long slide.

The others followed him. Then they found themselves in an immensely large hall, in which one could have safely let a thousand people sit at tables and with the ceiling no longer visible, the hall was bright as day, despite being illuminated by numerous torches that must have ignited themselves by a mechanism .

"Man, we have to be at least 800 meters under the ground, what work that must have cost," Ridschard stated with admiration.

"I want to know if they made the hallway that narrow to begin with or narrowed it down after the room?" asked Dan.

'What do you mean?' Jack asked back.

"If the first case applies, there's another way out of here. I don't know if I can pull myself up past the spears as fast as I fell." Dan.

"That's a good point, besides, it wouldn't have helped the others at the time either." replied Jack.

"Unless there was some mechanism to block them." objected Fed.

"That would be silly then the temple really is only for ship maps because you can't take anything up the low gears," added Simon.

"If you take the gold away from a god, for whom the temples were mostly built, what do you think would happen then?" said Dan.

"I think he's right the temples weren't built to extract gold just to leave it there. Which of course wasn't always an obstacle," said Jack.

"But there is no safe way among the Israelites, who at the Lord's command broke up the granaries for the offerings of the Lord and gave them to their people to eat." improved spring

"Let's go ahead and find out." Ridschard.

They went into a passage that was behind some kind of altar. It was a table composed of two ivory arches, in which rested a marble slab inlaid with gold designs. The slab was about 3 x 4 m in size and without any sacrificial signs from the past except oil.

"Here," shouted Simon, who of course found the gold first.

They came to a room full of chests containing pearls, gems, or gold items.

"Don't take any gold with you, it's too heavy, we've got enough stuff here," Dan called, thinking about the way back.

Everyone grabbed the pearls and jewels and lined their pockets.

Suddenly Fed shouted, "We have to get out of here. The room is getting lower."

Ridschard jumped up and hit his head hard, he was a big man.

"You convinced me," Simon said and sprinted into another aisle.

What the other signalless followed.

"Oooh, haaa," he suddenly came sprinting back, covered in mud.

"There are crocodiles." Simon.

"Okay, we're getting a little closer to the entrance." François

Everyone turned to François, "What?"

"Well, that's what's always at the beginning, spiders, snakes, crocodiles, skeletons, isn't." François

"Then two points we don't have any maps yet and maybe we can find a way without the lovely little animals please." Jack didn't like the thought of having to pass the animals at all.

Dan took a big diamond and his compass, stomped off and said, "where there are animals there is light."

"Oh, poor crocodiles," said Ernesto.

"What, poor crocodiles, we have to go after him and stop him or help him." replied Jack.

"Do you remember what I said about how he drove the lions away." Ernesto.

They laughed, everyone knew the story.

When they arrived there were no crocodiles or water and Dan was sitting at the other end of the creek hollow.

"Where's the water?" asked Simon, puzzled.

"Accidentally (accidentally) disappeared, man I thought you weren't coming anymore" Dan.

"What do you mean accidentally disappeared." Jack

"The stupid crocodile was already out of the water, had turned around to flee because of the light reflection and smashed the tail of whatever it was. After that, gas began to escape from the hole, and all the water flowed that direction." Dan.

He pointed to an approximately 2 meter high and wide corridor through which light came in.

"Now we have two free aisles," Dan added.

"We don't have the maps yet, let's check this aisle first. Where the water flowed out and where the light came from should be one hundred percent the exit afterwards," said Ridschard.

"You're the boss," Dan replied, walking on.

"Isn't he scared at all?" asked Simon.

"No only that you don't come home safely," his father answered him.

"What? Why me?" Simon.

"Because he feels responsible." Fed.

After a few turns of the corridor, they came into a hall full of blocks, huge clay tablets and murals.

"Well, we can't take them with us." Said Simon, "everything almost for nothing."

"Unfortunately, we don't take photos that have any color," the photographer said.

When they got to the last picture, the light from taking the picture was reflected very scattering.

The entrance closed behind them and a new corridor opened in front of them.

"That would make the creek bed obsolete as an exit, let's go there before it closes again." Said Ridschard and went through.

After about 20 meters, the entrance closed again, triggered by stepping on a stone slab that seemed to only be floating on the floor.

"We'd better stay together, who knows how many floodgates there are yet to come," said Fed promptly.

He had just spoken when the ground beneath them gave way and the slab of stone propelled by water at high speed shot down the passage.

"Wherever that takes us at the speed, it takes us days to get back to where we started," Ridschard said.

After quite a while, they broke out of a mountain outlet and fell horizontally in a river, with water lashing over them.

"Well I think we're out," Dan said, grinning after coming out of the water.

"yeah great just where is out there?" said Jack.

"Now that there is only one waterfall within about 2 months according to the map. I'd say by the river where I look twice before putting my hand in." Dan.

"Do you think we covered the whole distance, 3 and a half weeks in such a short time?" Ernesto

"No, must disappoint you just the same river, not the same place. But if we build a raft, we can do it in maybe four days."

"Why didn't we just take this route over water?" asked Ridschard.

"Well, we're not exactly in the desired area, we actually wanted to avoid the locals here." Dan.

"Then we shouldn't discuss so much and build the rafts." Fed replied and began to take his axe and chop down a tree.

They started cutting down the trees and only stopped when they felt they had have enough.

During the night they put up more guards - it remained quiet.

The natives showed good building skill, and by noon the rafts were made and launched.

The raft trip lasts 6 days because the amperage did not stay the same and often had to be paddled.

Despite the fresh coolness of the river air, the men were exhausted. They where now on the road for 2 months without making a major stop or simply stopping for a day and gathering new strength. They had kept their schedule short, having waited until the main dry season was over. Now that they didn't have to do almost anything, just paddle a little sometimes, they began to feel the strains of the past few weeks. Many also slept through the first 2 or 3 days if they didn't have to row.

Then it became more lively again, they looked at the drawings that had been made in the meantime and discussed the experiences in order to first record them in the form of notes.

Towards the end there was less talking again, except on the raft where the natives were, with whom Dan was temporarily and sometimes François as well. There they exchanged the wisdom of the different peoples.

"It is strange to see the contact between your town and the natives. I mean they're not like other slaves," Ridschard began to Fed.

"They aren't either." Fed.

"No what?" Ridschard.

"Not slaves and probably never will be until the end of Dan's generation." Fed.

"He has a lot of influence in the city huh?" Ridschard.

"Well, in some ways, yes, but that's not the reason." Fed.

Fed told how the Africans saved the lives of many children and probably some adults with water during the great drought.

"I see. - Don't you sometimes feel like coming to Europe again? visiting old friends, etc.?" Ridschard.

"In the beginning yes, or just visit friends and switch off. It has become less. My son grew up more here, the house, the friends here. We are at home here now, the people waiting for us when we leave the house or even the city are more here than in Europe. When we got on the ship and said goodbye, we had to be aware that we might not even have the opportunity to see each other again. Once you have received the blessing to go new ways of our own, you close the old chapter inside. You're also settling in, adapting to the new lifestyle. I think we would also be acting very strangely now in Europe. A lot comes from Europe to Africa to the cities, even the railways, but it remains different." Fed.

They continued to talk, and Ridschard told more about the latest changes in Europe.

On the sixth day they arrived at the place where they wanted to come down from the river to continue on the land. They had chosen a different position. They didn't have to climb up there.

"Now guys, let's continue on foot, it's time to stop lazy resting," Fed told the others.

"Too bad we're just starting to put up with it," Jack replied with a grin.

"I can really imagine that, but that's the way home," said Ridschard, pointing into the jungle.

"No there," Dan disagreed, pointing in the opposite direction.

The others laughed, it was a nice failure.

"Well, yes, we can go my own way and then arrive after a nice trip around the world, but I prefer the shorter route," Ridschard replied, adding with a laugh. "Although I would be up for a trip around the world another time. "He's never tired," Dan said, waving his hand, which started the laughter again.

attack in the dark

They took the rafts out of the water and laid them on the shore, not wanting to come back and hoping they would still be there. Simple, they didn't want to just let her float on the water and possibly jam something somewhere.

In the end they filled up their water supplies once more and set off.

The youth was fresh again, so the others heard them telling jokes again, and after a while they began to sing happily again. Dan loved it and was full of joy and energy again. He ran with his friend and often intoned a song, which made him the lead singer. Sometimes they sang in Swahili, sometimes in English.

Towards evening they set up a camp and it was obvious that most of them would stay up very late. The march had tired them, but the joy and cheerfulness was stronger through the songs during the day, so that they fell not asleep straight away. There wasn't much new to tell, after 2 months everything that felt worth telling had been exchanged. But something was always told, even if some of the stories were just a repetition.

After a few hours, even the last one could no longer stay awake and fell asleep.

So it was that the last night's watch fell asleep without a relief.

The next morning, Naomi and Dan didn't get up. They had been completely stunned and woven in during a nighttime tarantula attack. The guards had let the fire go out while falling asleep.

Horror and reproaches spread to James who had the last watch.

I didn't think they would dare get so close to groups of humans, or even that," said François.

"We don't know how many there were and no fire." replied Jack.

The men freed the two from the tissue. They were only breathing weakly.

"Let's give them coffee very strong and then let's get out of here, don't feel like waiting for them to come back," ordered Ridschard.

They forced the two to walk on their own feet, supported by the others, but also gave them a few breaks, being careful not to fall asleep.

When they finally left the jungle after three days, it wasn't as hot as when they started. It was mid-autumn and it made walking in the steppe a lot easier.

Nevertheless, after a few days the water began to run out - the two young men's detoxification had cost a lot of water.

In the evening Ridschard and Fed sat down to discuss the water situation.

"With a reduction in the water ration, we could still make it to the next water point on our route. But I don't think we can deal with the condition of the two of them. They still have a fever at times and need even more water than we do. If we take another water point 3-4 days from here, we will need about 5 to 6 days more. It's probably going to weigh on everyone a little more no matter

what we do, we doe just takes a little longer."
Explained Fed the situation.
"It's not really a question to decide. I think
we better take a few more days. Plus, I'm not
really convinced that anyone other than
Naomi and Dan would make it.
The natives, besides you, would probably be
the only ones who could really see a big
chance and conserve enough water to feed
the two of them."
"So shall we take the nearest lake to the
east?" Fed.
"Yes, I think we should. - If we keep it to
ourselves for the time being, the others will
still be a little frugal according to their
possibilities." Ridschard.
"Well we have to tell Dan anyway so he
doesn't correct us in front of the others." Fed.
"OK, let's tell him we're going to go to the
other lake just to make sure we have enough
water." Ridschard.
Then they went to sleep. The guards had
been doubled after the last incident so they
could keep each other awake.
The next morning, after Fed and Ridschard
talked to Dan, they went their different way
to the other lake. The others didn't notice
anything and the Africans guessed the reason
for this decision because they didn't say
anything.
"Man I never thought I'd miss the rain, back
home I could soon curse how often it comes
and here," Jack fumed.

"Well this is Africa, it doesn't rain for months," Fed replied, grinning, half laughing.
"Yes, but I've been here for half a year now and not a drop." Jack
"We'll get water." Fed.
"When?" Jack
"In four days," Ridschard replied, "please don't lose your nerve, Dan warned us before we went."
"No, don't worry, but it's still ironic." Jack
"So what are you going to do when we get home," Dan tried to change the subject.
"I'll go to my hotel room, hang up the Do Not Disturb sign, run myself a bath, and won't come out until my skin wrinkles." replies Jack.
They laughed but didn't think it was a bad idea.
"Yes, I think so, too, and then I would order a >> good one << and slowly let it go glass by glass," said Ernesto.
"If you were just drinking wine, I would keep you company," admitted François.
"A, maybe I'll take a chance, but then it has to be a really good one." Ernesto.
"Oh, that's almost an insult, we French are born experts." François
"Alcoholic," Dan commented.
"Well, no talk of it, but we know what YOUR first action will be after the bath."
"Oh, the type of bath is important. I would go in the water with her." Dan.
"L'amure." François

"Man, I'm glad we got your own bathroom done before then," said Fed, laughing.

"But Ernesto, you don't need to take a hotel room for the bathroom, I can wait until your skin is crumpled." François

Suddenly the group stopped and the porters stopped.

"I'll see what's up," Dan said, stepping forward. Fed and Ridschard followed him.

There was no panic to be felt, so they assumed there was no danger, but there was some information.

There were tracks that indicated that lions had attacked a rhino there the previous day. They examined if there was any sign that the rhino was sick. So that the lions attacked it despite its size. But there was no sign to be found.

"OK let's move on, keep your eyes open and spread with your guns a bit," said Fed with Dan and Ridschard agreeing.

Three days later in the morning, one of the Africans asked Dan to come to Naomi.

He knew what was to come, Naomi felt worse again yesterday and he didn't feel as strong anymore either.

Dan followed him without asking or saying anything.

"I'm sorry," Dan said upon seeing Naomi.

"No, there is no reason to. Thank you for the years you gave me. Without you I would have died from the leg infection. I still had beautiful wonderful years." Naomi

"It was Nadiene. - But it's still my fault if I had... I don't know." Dan.
"No it wasn't your fault you didn't have a guard and it got us both and I'm just not as strong as you.
The spirits wanted me before, then they let me, I thank you for that. Now it's time." Naomi.
"No," Dan yelled, his eyes filled with tears. "Please, you have to promise me to keep living for both of us."
"I will keep our bond, your two wives will stay with me." Dan.
"Tell them I said not to refuse another man when the time is up, please look they are still young, they can still get married." Naomi
"I'll take care of everything." Dan.
Naomi no longer answers, he had died.
They buried him and stayed in silence for a while.

The Homecoming

They reached the lake in the evening, but Fed and Dan stopped them from drinking.
In the lake swam a half decomposed wildebeest.
"We boil the water," Fed said.
"Will that be enough?" asked Ridschard.

"We have no choice, the nearest water source is 10 days away and we are out of water now," Dan replied.

"I'm sorry, it seems we haven't just signed off on an expedition." Ernesto.

"What are you talking about just because an animal is decomposing in the water, that happens more often here." Dan.

Dan went to boil water, he didn't want to talk about the other accidents.

They fished the animal out of the water, burned it and staked the skull on it.

It was three more weeks before the native village, which was the first on their way, could be seen.

With the sight of their home, the Africans began to sing again. They also sang a song about defying the spirits of death. They started out in Swahili, but since Dan didn't mind in the least, they continued singing in English.

They stopped there and accepted an invitation to a meal.

But since Dan didn't want to stay that long, they were invited to the homecoming party the next evening.

Then they went on together. Now only a few Africans came along. It was only those needed for the burdens to be carried. Since everyone carried as much as they could carry, it was down to two and Dan's best friends who would have done it even for free if Ridschard had allowed it.

After two hours, 10 meters from the city, the first people came towards them and took some luggage from them.

On the outskirts of town, Jenny came up to them with Chris and Nadiene's mother to greet them.

"Where's Nadiene?" Dan immediately asked, a little nervous.

"She's got a surprise for you," Jenny replies, taking his backpack from him, knowing he's about to run.

And he did wrestle. But suddenly he stopped behind him, a familiar voice had said, Papa. He turned around, "Chris."

Jenny and Nadiene's mother were also surprised. "Nadiene practiced with him for the whole three months to surprise you, but he didn't want to," Jenny said.

Dan picked him up and said, "yeah dad's here." He held him tightly to himself, then he left, but faster, to see Nadiene.

When he saw Nadiene he knew what was happening.

"I only half understood my son when he said papa." Dan.

"Oh the rascal all the time I try and he doesn't say it once." Nadine

"Well look, he's right, papa can only be one, he can't call you papa." Dan.

"Yes, yes!" Nadiene.

"Have you been to the doctor?" Dan.

"Yes. - It was our last night - it will come in spring." Nadiene.

This calls for celebrations Dan.
They held each other for a while after the
others had arrived.

END

Afterword

This story is not based on truth historical
fact.
All technical actions are possible except for
the fire in the temple, but it is not advisable
to try them all yourself.
For studies on the animals and African
weather patterns, the German Brockhaus and
German Universal Dictionary by Brockhaus
were used.
But most of all the book was written to make
you enjoy reading it.

Raginmund

Manufacturing and Publishing:

BoD: Books on Demand, Norderstedt
ISBN 9783837059175

© 2022 Raginmund
all copy right infos by Sabam.be